Ticket To A Lonely Town

Bruce Henricksen

Ticket To A Lonely Town

Bruce Henricksen

a collection of stories

ATOMIC QUILL PRESS

Ticket To A Lonely Town

ISBN 0-9760535-3-5

Published by Atomic Quill Press

Atomic Quill Press
P.O. Box 39859
Detroit, MI 48239
press.atomicquill.com

design + layout: ledaddyswing

Distributed by Pathway Book Service
1.800.345.6665 • pbs@pathwaybook.com

Printed in the United States

To
Viki

Acknowledgments

Literary magazines that published early versions of these stories are *Arts & Letters, The Barcelona Review, The Briar Cliff Review, Folio, Full Circle Journal, New Orleans Review, The New Review of Literature, North Dakota Quarterly, Southern Humanities Review, and Tulane Review.* Two of these stories have been anthologized, one in *French Quarter Fiction* (Light of New Orleans) and another in *Mota 4: Integrity* (Triple Tree). The editors of these publications have helped prepare this collection, which Timothy Dugdale of Atomic Quill Media has brought to life.

Many people have given me advice about individual stories and about the craft of writing. These include Jill Adams, Robert Olen Butler, Peggy Downing, Viki Henricksen, Timothy Magee, Joseph Maiolo, Janet Nelson, Eric Nystrom, Cheryl Reitan, and Barton Sutter. I'm especially grateful to three stalwarts who earned stars in their crowns by writing detailed comments on the entire manuscript: Anthony Bukoski, Ted Cotton, and my daughter, Jessica Henricksen. The Duluth Writers' Workshops, administered by Joseph Maiolo, have been an inspiration to me and to many others in this area. And I've been encouraged by the interest and support of my dear friends Paul Decker and Kitty O'Keefe.

Ticket to a Lonely Town is dedicated to my wife, Viki, who saved my life years ago and has enriched it each day since.

Contents

The Night, the Stars

Everyone is ashamed of something, but my memories fill me with shame. Some people say that memories can be untrue, and that would be okay with me.

Mine crowd me, unpleasant and insistent, and I wish I could believe that they're unreal. In any case, we *are* our memories, and this story is an interview with mine. Don't ask why these and not others; they have a will of their own, like creatures rising from psychic mud. But a story is like the splashes of a stone that you skip a few feet out onto the sea—the memories it touches are microscopic, and the great whole dreams along undisturbed. Each of us exceeds his story.

In the Oak Street Bookstore, a brindling shotgun house in the University District, the air conditioning was broken and the overhead fan turned languidly. August in New Orleans. I was poking in the mystery section and tossing glances out the dusty window and beyond the rooftops at clouds gathering north of the city, over Lake Pontchartrain. Tough, dark clouds. Clouds in filthy jeans and hooded sweats. Clouds that had parked their Harleys and were ambling toward town, meaning business. There was thunder in the distance, like a rack of pool balls rolling down the chute. Just as the afternoon was going all James Lee Burke, a vice crushed something in my chest. A professorial type with a kid in tow watched me fall. My last thought was that my head had split on the floor and its nasty secrets, packed together like worms in a fisherman's can, were squirming about in the aisle.

Florence Tsu was part of the mess on the floor, the first slap of the pebble on the sea. I had hoisted Florence into bed decades before, wet and wiggling as any trout. Then one morning I was standing by the kitchen sink—the scene is Los Angeles now—splitting an English muffin and spooning strawberry jam onto the halves. Someone on the radio was singing "In My Solitude." Barb had done laundry, and on the clothesline outside the window a happy crew of blouses and pants jitterbugged to a different tune.

"Interesting." It was Barbara behind me. I turned to see her holding a long, black hair up to the light. Barbara had Brigitte Bardot lips, brown hair, and silver, laser-beam eyes that stunned her audiences when she sang. That morning she fired them at me—waves of resentment and particles of reproach—as I stood there in my Jockeys with my muffin by the dripping faucet.

"A friend of mine saw you in Westwood with an Asian girl." As Joplin, the cat, did figure eights between her legs, Barbara wound the souvenir from Florence about her finger and placed it in a jewelry case. The memory is still vivid, its choreography—the hair turning slowly about her finger, to be encased like a relic, Ellington's "Solitude," the jiving laundry, Joplin turning on the floor, the silver eyes. I don't remember what followed. The scene vaporizes and slips away like stage mist into the wings.

It was the decade of Timothy Leary and SNCC, of love-ins and psychedelia, of "groovy" and "where it's at." I was a grad student, teaching first semester history at UCLA, and Barb sang lead in an all-girl band. I first spotted her on Santa Monica Boulevard after one of her gigs, a SNCC benefit at the Troubadour, sashaying along in a red mini-skirt tight as an Ace bandage. It was a warm July night filled with traffic and a light breeze off the Pacific. 1967, the year of Sergeant Pepper.

"I want to get lost in your rock and roll," I said, falling in beside her. It was a line that ended up in a hit song. She tossed her brown hair into the breeze and smiled, then we went to Barney's for a beer. Later that night we walked barefoot on Zuma Beach, Barb's hair thrashing in the wind under brilliant stars. It was the

Summer of Love. Soon LBJ, defeated and dour, would quit the field, Bobby Kennedy would be shot by Sirhan Sirhan, and the nation would elect Nixon and Agnew. But what I remember most of that gone decade is the Summer of Love.

Barb and I rented a precarious little house, not much bigger than the snail-back trailer that I lived in as a child in Minneapolis. The house was on a hillside in Echo Park, a neighborhood that was half Chicanos and broken Chevies, half peaceniks and VW buses. Streets looped and wound through the hills, and it was seventy steps down through a thicket to our house, which had an avocado tree and a fish pond just off the front porch. Barb hung a basket-chair from a branch by the pond. It was a secret garden in the city, where, with an album of Joan Baez or Bob Dylan coming to us through an open window and the smell of jasmine all around, we watched the smog turn pink in the setting sun and breathed the lovely, poisoned air. We had been married eight months when I decided to sniff-out the moist pleasures of Florence, one of my students.

When, two years later, Tulane offered me a job, we loaded the VW bus, scraped off the *We Shall Overcome* and *Make Love Not War* bumper stickers, and moved the show to New Orleans. But after the third year, Tulane flushed me. My book wasn't happening, and stories of my actual nocturnal accomplishments had propagated like fleas about administrative ears. Barbara sang in New Orleans clubs for a few years, rubbing elbows with the Nevilles at Tipatina's and jamming with Ellis Marsalis at Snug Harbor, while I drank in smoky neighborhood dives, shagging stray bimbos or working on my pool game among old men whose eyes had gone vacant behind bottles. Sometimes I'd meet Barb after a gig and we'd walk home in the indigo night along sodden streets that smelled of yesterdays, feeling our lives drifting like debris in a deep-sea current.

In my spare time, I peddled balloons to car dealers along Veterans Boulevard. Not really, but that's how insignificant life seemed. The Sixties were over. Eventually Barb turned to social work, trading in mini-skirts, bell-bottoms, and tie-dyes for garb more appropriate to a white person braving the New Orleans projects to counsel illiterate women about child care and drug abuse.

On the Coast, I'd been a member of CORE, blue-jeaned and bearded, with hair politically abundant. I chanted slogans at marches and spent a month walking a petition around Watts to end de facto segregation in the public schools. Feeling alive, with bone and muscles and the possibility of action, I schmoozed with James Farmer as we picketed the Goldwater convention at the Cow Palace in San Francisco in '64. Later, reinventing my act in the classrooms of Tulane, I talked about writing a history of the protest movement in the Sixties—of Mario Salvio and H. Rap Brown, The Freedom Singers, The Weathermen. I was clean shaven, with hair trimmed to above the collar, and the book would scratch my name at least into a footnote of academic history. A professional rememberer, I'd be remembered.

But my ideals had crumbled like dead leaves, and my writing was haunted by sarcasm and sniggers. The blunder in Vietnam had unraveled in an undignified scramble to helicopters and dinghies, and civil rights here at home was a dead issue. At least to me. In New Orleans, the black people living down every street meant guns and violence. There were rude clerks in every supermarket and ruder panhandlers in every parking lot. The geographical distance between the races, upon which so much high sentiment depends, was obliterated in New Orleans. From my bedroom at night, I'd hear the black voices in the street, voices enveloping the house in a murky terrain of dark, drawling valleys and sharp, falsetto peaks. Then, in the morning, Colt 45 cans, spilling from their brown-bag sleeves, decorated the gutters and lawns—the black aesthetic. And from their progeny, Doritos bags everywhere—in the azaleas, under the crepe myrtles, and kited by gusts into the Spanish moss that dripped from live oaks. Doritos: Breakfast of Pickaninnies. It was a slovenly culture of resentment that slowly strangled sympathy.

I couldn't write about Rap Brown or Angela Davis without a snicker slipping through the picket fence of words. I became one of those people over thirty that we had sworn, in our marching days, never to trust. Curiously, it was Barbara who became the historian, struggling to recover something of the Sixties, retreating to her improvised carrel in a far corner of the house and surrounding herself with documents from that gone decade—my old copy of *The Port Huron Statement*, tattered back issues of *Ramparts* and I.F. Stone's *Newsletter*, and once vibrant books like Eldridge Cleaver's *Soul on Ice*, books that had turned to gravestones in my hands. To Barbara, these small, tumbling stacks on the desk and floor were a jagged fortress against time. But I was through with history. If I read at all back then, stretched on the sofa in front of the TV—while Nixon, Ford, and Carter waved, stumbled and smiled away the years—it was to tag along with fictional detectives like Philip Marlowe or Travis McGee. Some days I forgot to shave.

The Movement, which careened through the Sixties on rails named Alabama and Vietnam, had given me structure, a selfhood. Politics does that—the strategy sessions, the books, the sit-ins and marches. But now I was giving anarchy a try. Not consciously, of course. Most of life is not driven by consciousness. You don't sit back and say, *this is what I'll become.* Instead you merely notice one day, *oh, this is what I am now.* And it isn't a matter of liking what you see. In New Orleans I lived for the clamor of the bars—for the buzz, the feel of smoke in my lungs, the sexual ambushes. Marriages flamed out around us, as ours rotted its steady "The Snows of Kilimanjaro" rot.

❁

Barb and I were brought together for a while in the Seventies by the suicide of an old friend, Phil Ochs, and by the birth of our son, Jagger. Phil hanged himself in a loft in New York, depressed that he couldn't write songs anymore, songs like the one we had admired that toked-up night in Los Angeles when we met him at the Ash Grove, the words of his song so new that he had them spread out on a chair on the stage:

Soon your sailing will be over.
Come and take the pleasures of the harbor.

But the memories that took the dance floor when Phil died shuffled back into the shadows. When I picture him now, his face drifts out of focus. By the end of the Seventies, Barb and I had become like bloated corpses in the harbor Phil had sung about, minor casualties of the decade of love and flowers.

Suddenly there was Velcro, then AIDS. *Wow* gave way to *awesome*, and Datsuns became Nissans. In jazz joints and oyster bars, people talked personal computers and mutual funds. Jagger was in school, slouching his vanguard slouch toward the dark prison of adolescence, that black hole from which no message escapes. With a flick of the wrist, time toppled the Berlin Wall and sent the Evil Empire sprawling. Around town, yuppies pounded jogging trails and gentrified houses. Others dyed their hair purple and green or shaved their heads bald, and rings dangled by the fistful from noses and ears, eyebrows and lips. A new image repertoire was in place. Gays were marching, Clinton's dong was in the news, and privacy had gone public. I hadn't dropped acid in twenty-five years.

I don't know why I recall these moments—the discovered souvenir from Florence, the night by the sea, Barbara's carrel in New Orleans, the news of Phil's death—and not others. You fling your stone side-arm at the sea, and it nicks the surface where it will.

One appropriately rainy afternoon—Barbara's mother had died—Barb and Jagger dragged an old suitcase through a ticket line and boarded a Greyhound to Idaho and the funeral. After dropping them at the station, I popped some breath mints and navigated our Ford Escort through half-submerged streets to the French Quarter. The bimbo I snagged after two or three bars was named Cookie, or Candy—something edible—a hairdresser with gallons of bazooms, scarlet lips, a nose tending toward honker, and long curls that spilled in my hands like the Slinkies of childhood. By 2 a.m. we had traversed the flooded city and became snakes tangled in our bed, Barb's and mine. But dealing with a bimbo in the morning was always a messy job, like cleaning fish. You wondered if it was worth it. After marching Cookie out into the subsiding waters, I checked the bedding for hairs, lipstick stains, blood—the usual. I hadn't told her that I was married, and she'd been too sloshed to notice.

So the succubus from the Quarter, oblivious to the ethics of the one-nighter, sashayed by our peeling shotgun house on Laurel Street a couple of weeks later. Barbara and I were having brunch in the kitchen, muffins and strawberry jam, as the radio played and Slick, the cat, dozed in a patch of sunlight. In butt-crushing jeans, her Slinky-toy curls bouncing, Cookie strolled through the back door, open for the breeze. I walked her up through the house and out onto the front porch. Instead of a shotgun, it was Barbara's ray-gun eyes scorching my back all the guilty, pathetic way.

"Can't you see that you're killing me?" Barbara asked, eyes grazing mine. They were tired of everything, those eyes, and gravity had done a number on her face. "Can't you see that . . . ." I don't know what she was about to say—the word took root like a cancer on her tongue. After a while I heard, "Jesus, Hugh, brush your teeth once in a while. How do the whores stand you?"

"They're not whores," I muttered.

"And when did you get so pathetic?"

For a moment I tried to answer the question, to produce a date or event. Then a car backfired down the pot-holed street, the familiar belch-and-fart of city life. When I shuffled home from the Dew Drop Inn late that night, wondering if she'd locked me out, I found her in her carrel doing weed and staring at the multicolored galaxies, comets, and nebulae of the screen saver.

A few days later I plopped myself down in a marriage counselor's office in the Riverbend, shifting my fattening ass about in a fake-leather chair that squatted among potted plants and museum posters. It's strange how, when you're getting your teeth drilled or your botched life dissected, there has to be art everywhere. When Meg Burton, the counselor, offered cappuccino, I flashed on being in Hollywood, where everyone schmoozes and networks in sidewalk cafes, where everyone does therapy and is blithely on the mend.

But I knew that it wouldn't work. Barb and I were stuck with what we were. If the old heavyweights—The Church, The Family, and The Self-Help Book—had lost their punches, what would this skinny counselor accomplish? Not that I actually read self-help books, or went to church either. I was skeptical about this whole self-knowledge concept, since the knower and the known are the same self. It makes no sense, like a ruler measuring itself.

Meg was all optimism, a kid fresh out of grad school, perky and businesslike with note pad and an old tape recorder and eyes big as oysters on the half shell. It was the first session, where she talked to us separately. I gazed out of the second-floor window and past the joggers on the levee, where black kids flung stones at a dog. She asked me to say something about myself. I told her that I'd seen fire, I'd seen rain. Regrets, I'd had a few.

We circled around to my drinking, and I thought about my dad, slouching at bars in various dingy neighborhoods in Minneapolis during my trailer-park childhood, clutching his bottle as you might clutch a utility pole in a hurricane. I remembered bumping awake to the shaking of the trailer as he banged to get in on a cold November night when my mother, tired and desperate, had locked him out. In the morning, as I left for school, I found him huddled on the ground near a garbage can, rubbing his legs together like a fly. “What do you think of your mother locking your dad out like this?” he whined.

I had always wanted to talk to him in later years, to ask him *why*, but he had vanished, returning only to claw about sometimes in memory’s crawl spaces. For years, I had a dream where he stood with his back to me in an unknown city gazing at a wall covered with wildstyle graffiti that I couldn’t read. Then he’d disappear around a corner, turning at the last instant to glance back at me through dreamspace with a face as featureless as a cheap balloon.

Of course the dream is a distortion. But the other memories? Dad shivering by the garbage can? The shaking trailer? Have I made my father into an excuse, reshaping him like a mad scientist in the mind’s underground lab? I don’t think so, but . . . .

I told Meg about my favorite booth by the window of Sheri’s Saloon in the Irish Channel. About how I liked sitting under the orange neon sign, the layers of smoke drifting across the pool table and in front of the juke, a bimbo across the table sipping a beer. I wove a scene out of Kinky Friedman, supposedly fraught with the meaning of life—a scene with a beauty as fake as the starlight that fell from the ceilings of movie palaces when I was a kid. I told her about the sad-eyed regulars, craftsmen of the bottle and the glass, each reliving in his mind his own little story. I told how, for a while, a good saloon is a place outside of time. But inevitably, as the blaring mornings crash through windows, the nights’ visions curdle into caustic slime under the rims of eyes.

But Meg merely took notes—she was a good little note taker—and asked if I’d thought of finding something else to fill my time. Like maybe she featured me as a shutterbug, or a philatelist with albums and magnifying glass. Her question made me feel utterly alone. Life was textured with such moments of solitude.

Through the open window of her office I listened to the hum and clatter of tires on asphalt, the incessant sigh and groan of the everyday. Boredom, I think, was the father of all my sins. I tried not to stare at Meg's skinny legs that jutted out of her skirt like chop sticks. She shifted the pad to her other thigh and squinted her oyster eyes. "When couples are having trouble, Hugh, it's important for them to remember what first brought them together. What was it that attracted you to Barbara . . . that made you want to marry her?"

Out on the levee, the black kids and the targeted dog had disappeared. Answering Meg's question was like trying to read the smoke of a poem you've burned. I thought about Zuma Beach and the sound of the surf beneath silent stars, stars behind stars. About Barbara's hair rising in the wind by the undulating sea—in the salt air smelling of millennia. Her Bardot lips. And how, holding Barbara's hand that night as we walked in the sand, separated by a slice of wind, we had talked about the sky being layers of time, all the times of the universe, and how the galaxies gaze at us from billions of years ago. The memory of that night hadn't returned in a decade, but it hadn't died either.

"Hugh, if you could say something to Barbara that you haven't been able to say, what would it be?"

Nothing came to mind but the immortal words of Jerry Lee Lewis: shake it one time for me. On the wall a cockroach listened, brown and shiny and waving antennae that you could hook to your Sony. Among her potted plants and posters, the roach looking on, Meg, who didn't pack many laughs, continued to nail me down in her notes, her own invisible antennae raking the air. She looked at me, and I lowered my eyes. My socks didn't match. What is it about being seen? About women's eyes? Some guys thrive on a woman's gaze, guys posing in bars, drinking in the looks like a sponge. With me, if they looked too close, their eyes became halogen lamps and I shriveled like a zapped bug.

The counseling didn't accomplish much. As I said, I was convinced that at a certain point your texture of being hardens, and all of the possible selves that you once slipped on and off so easily have disappeared like clothing lost at the laundromat. You're naked and skinny and all that you'll ever be. But now

I'm not so sure that's true. Maybe people aren't simply the sum of their acts or their memories. Maybe we are always an open potential. But after a life like mine, what is salvaged with this new philosophy? What is absolved?

Barb and I stuck it out, mainly to get Jagger through school. Eventually, he dropped out of UNO, stuffed a few things in a duffel bag, and pointed his old Corolla toward Alaska. I remember standing sometimes in his room, where he'd left his skateboard and some posters of sleek cars and swimsuit babes slowly peeling from the wall. I'd try to reconstruct his misplaced childhood, remembering only fragments, only specks of time—the dead hamster, the stolen bike, the cheeks glazed with tears. And the girl he brought home one evening, lovely and shy as a butterfly.

When Barbara died, plopping forward into her clam spaghetti as I gazed out the kitchen window wondering who'd be at the Dew Drop Inn later that evening, I tried to contact Jagger. A voice arrived through phlegm and vast circuitry: "That skinny kid that used to stumble around with the music turned up loud all night? Said his mom played rock and roll? We got rid of him months ago."

So Jagger's trail had gone cold. Like my father, he had sunk beneath the surface, lost in my story's submerged cities, as I'll be lost in his.

The cremation was a desperate little affair, tinged with a kind of Sixties trippiness. The funeral parlor on Dryades Street, a converted home of sagging floors set up on blocks against God's muddied waters, served the black community—an old house with afterburners added in back to blast souls heavenward. Reverend Leon was huge and vague behind a battered desk in an office filled with cigar smoke that probably dated back to the Great

Depression. His what-the-fuck look hung in the haze as I leaned in the skewed doorway and asked about prices. But it turned out that he had heard of Barb's work in the community, so we struck a deal. I fed him some data on her life, and we did the funeral three days later.

I brought a bouquet of lilies, and Reverend Leon hauled out some plastic flowers from the storeroom. Barbara and I hadn't had many friends. One couple she had kept in touch with from my Tulane days showed up, as did a frump in a purple dress from the social services office, a witch, really, with makeup stirred together in a vat. And there was Stan, one of my nightlife cronies, bleary and wasted, filling his little corner of the chapel with Stan fumes, the familiar Stan exhaust, rumored to have killed insects. But fifteen to twenty black folks came, mostly women Barb had helped at one time or another, gussied up in hats and veils.

The Reverend, brown and shining like a polished shoe, puffed himself up and intoned into the desolate chapel. He was James Earl Jones telling how Barbara Talbot had made music on the stage and then in the lives of God's unfortunate children, saying how she had kept the faith and was now joining God's choir, where she would sing forever. Someone muttered amen into the subliminal breeze descending from the ceiling fan, and I flashed on Barbara up in some heavenly dive in her mini-skirt, jamming with Phil Ochs, rubbing the Fender into her crotch before a flock of boogying angels—angels with Day-Glo flowers painted on their cheeks and boobs, doing blow and flinging themselves about like rag dolls. An eternal '67—The Summer of Love expanding into the galaxies and across eternity. My celestial trip in the style of *Laugh-In* was interrupted when Leon gave the signal and they fired up the burners.

After the service I made straight for the door, but a crooked old woman with a small, curio face dragged herself—I thought of a rat gassed by Stan—in front of me to say how Barbara had saved her daughter from drugs and poverty and how the Lord would surely welcome her into His arms. By the door Stan, who had apparently started something, was sullen in his vapors, swaying like a small boat on the uneven floor, his exit from the harbor blocked by a battleship of a woman with hands on hips.

"Yo! Don't you be puttin' no badmouth on me. You hear? You comin' here all shitface. Later wi' chyou!"

"Gassman," I said, passing by.

"Hugh."

Across the street an old Buick, its hood propped ajar with a board, coughed and wheezed into the baffled face of its owner. By the curb, a dead food can swelled like a corpse. July was boiling away.

In a couple of weeks, and after another sameshit night that I ornamented by blowing biscuits in the john of Sheri's at 3 a.m., I decided to hit on Courtney, who managed the Oak Street Bookstore. What was I thinking? That this spiffy, thirty-something chick would moisten up for a farting drunk with swizzle stick arms, boiled eyes, and raw meat for a face? A drunk crooning his sorrows through teeth the color of old piano keys? Yes, that's what I was thinking.

So with *The Lady in the Lake* in hand, sweating in the August heat, half of the gulf of Mexico sloshing in the New Orleans air, I brushed past the professor and his son, nauseated by the kid's stare, by the kid eyes beaming up from under a Cubs cap. I heard him whisper, "Daddy, that man smells like Buffy's doodies." The last words I heard when I occupied space and reflected light: *that man smells like Buffy's doodies*. I wanted to say something to the kid, to defend those who don't fit into the clean world, who wallow and stagger but feel most alive in the air cobwebbed by cigarette smoke and the smells of spilled beer and cheap perfume. But it was too late. Outside, the badass-biker clouds rumbled in. Then the vise closed in my chest, the worm-secrets slithered on the floor, and I tumbled down the dark river toward my sea of memories.

You stand on a shore, balancing a stone in your hand. Then you fling it sidearm. It skips a small way out onto the surface of the sea, and after the final splash it sinks. The surface is smooth again. The ending of a story is that stone sinking into the unsaid.

And what would I say to you, Barbara, if saying were possible now—if dust could speak to smoke? I wouldn't deny these memories, my derelicts, but I'd say that I was a fool not to know that we're always unfinished and free. I would tell you that I'm ashamed. I wish that we could slip back, as on a trail of ancient starlight falling through time, and begin the story again by the avocado tree and the fish pond in Echo Park in what they called The Summer of Love. I regret the heart's abandoned work. I'm sorry that things were rough for Jagger, and I thank you, Barbara, for tolerating me for all those years that we lived in our bodies and were responsible.

All those years that I'd slouch in Sheri's in front of ashtrays like bombed-out trailer parks and think about finding my father among the elders of the drinking tribe. I would imagine—I never told you this—I'd imagine flying back in time to search his fugitive haunts on the bleary skids of Washington Avenue or on lower Hennepin with its strip joints, in the old Minneapolis of my childhood. Maybe it's late on a windy Saturday afternoon in early November, circa 1950. Scraps tumble along the streets, mirroring the swift, high clouds. The bums worry about winter, gathering in doorways to talk about freight trains and journeys, their dusty underground language punctuated by the squeak of corks in bottles, their arms moving for warmth like damaged wings.

In this fantasy my father and I huddle in an old wooden booth by a window that frames a neon sign. The booth is a mausoleum, its memoried surfaces emblazoned with cigarette burns and carved everywhere with names and dates that ripple beneath the touch. We sense the lonely beauty wrought by time passing in derelict places, of disparate lives imploding to form a text, a history. Outside, the sky grows dark as any sea. Perhaps the clouds separate from time to time to reveal the ancient starlight, the worlds beyond worlds and the layers of time beyond need.

In the orange glow of the neon, I sit across the scarred table from my father. Billy Eckstine sings "In My Solitude" on the juke. I'm home. I buy my father a beer and crack the cellophane on a pack of Luckies. We talk, slowly releasing the past from its silence. I ask him if the drinking life began for him, as it did for me, with the thrill of sex lacing the smoke of jazz clubs and pool halls. Or maybe for him it started with terror in the carnage of the war—his war—now over. Contemplative behind his Lucky, matching his words to the currents of longing that all drinkers ride, he tells his story. As the neon flickers, we drink, taken by absence and desire, our bodies at rest in the void, our lives turning away from the world like motes drifting from a shaft of light. We carve our names. But we cannot speak, since death is the end of voice. And yet he haunts me, Barbara, as you do, with memories that will not die.

Gliders

The morning sunlight warms the breakfast room with its familiar aura of honey and peaches, and Bob Edwards is his friendly old self on Public Radio. But today Blake feels "different," as they say in Minnesota. It doesn't help that the view through the window is as fine as ever, that the remaining clouds are brilliant against a blue sky as they drift over Lake Superior toward Wisconsin. Or that the pine trees all down the hillside are brushed with fresh snow, plumes of powder floating from their branches and swirling away in the wind. All along the street, the porches and hedges have been transformed into reefs sunken beneath motionless waves of snow, even though the snowscape is already marred by footprints and tire tracks. Soon the snowplow will scrape the streets, sidewalks will be shoveled, and yards will erupt in children's forts and snowmen, the entire pristine scene dissolving into a crumpled text, a history of the day's work and play.

For Blake, during the past three years in Duluth, the year's first snowfall has conjured pleasant memories of childhood, although this morning the memories remain irritatingly remote. Not that he spends a lot of time in the mossy ruins. But for the past week he hasn't felt right, has felt different, and this morning his throat has gone raw and tight. Each breath slides down like gravel. He had hoped to share the first snowfall with his wife, Sandy, but he has been alone for three days as she visits her father in Minneapolis. A month ago she won a battle with her sister for power of attorney, a battle Blake had tried to ignore, and now her father is dying in University Hospital.

Being alone is bad enough, Blake thinks, but then to be sick and snubbed by one's own memories. Even the sight of a child playing in the snow fails to focus the truant scenes of his own childhood in Iowa, scenes that hover about the perimeters of consciousness. The child's head, wrapped in a red stocking cap, bounces about behind a snowdrift down the alley across the street. Like a bobber when there's a nibble, Blake thinks. All autumn long the child, not old enough for school, played alone at his "sky-blue trades" in the backyard, kicking around in the leaves that settled to the ground so inevitably and beautifully from a large maple.

As a boy, Blake lived with his grandparents in Del Mar, a bottom-line farm town lost between two hills in southern Iowa, a thousand miles from any sea. Where did the town's name come from? His mother pursued a career in Des Moines, his father having left them in favor of hoisting glasses and, from all reports, fumbling with bras and panties. *Good riddance to bad rubbish,* Blake's grandmother once said of his father as Blake played with Lincoln Logs in the next room. He was a useless man, Blake thinks, hardly worth damning. Blake wonders if, in his own way, he has become useless too.

Summer and winter until he was ten, Blake wandered Del Mar with no more supervision than the shiners in the creek. But that was decades ago, and things were different then—a child shouldn't kick around outdoors alone in these fallen days.

Blake turns away from the window and selects two vitamin C and two Advil from the pill bottles on the table. "These might help," he says aloud. Speaking to himself is a recent development, and the sound of his own voice startles him. Then, as he rises and walks toward the kitchen for a glass of water, something glides noiselessly into the basement stairway and out of sight.

During these three days alone, as autumn spun itself in a blur into winter, Blake has become increasingly aware of the soundless figures that lurk just on the edge of his vision, observing him. When he turns to look, they vanish, slipping behind a door or around a corner, avoiding confrontation like frightened deer. After his aged mother lost her eyesight a few years ago, she talked about "seeing" someone always with her, just off her left shoulder, but the doctor assured her that the explanation was physiological.

But Blake isn't sure how to explain his own visitors. It's easier to believe in the reality of these figures, even as science fiction beings from some twilight dimension or as—perish the thought—angels, than to contemplate the medical alternative. His mother had lived alone and blind for a year in her small apartment in Des Moines, bumping into furniture and surviving falls in the congealed light, accepting food and assistance from neighbors, until finally, frail as mist in the valley, she was hospitalized and died of brain cancer amid beeps and a tangle of tubes.

He had been her only remaining relative, but his position as a professor of literature at Tulane University in New Orleans had made it impossible for him to care for her as he had wanted to. Perhaps Blake's gliders are the start of a similar journey. It's a fear that has begun to awaken and stir in the basement of his mind.

Either his gliders are real—perhaps beings that whisper just out of earshot about our lives—or they're what his colleagues in the sciences call "instrument artifacts," false data produced by the measuring device, in this case the brain or eye. The thought that they're real is absurd, and the other thought is worse. Maybe that's why he found himself the other day, literally found himself, in the New Age section of Barnes & Noble leafing through a book on the occult. He looked about guiltily, like a man in a trench coat reading pornography, and replaced the book on the shelf, reminding himself of his scorn for all of the props and characters of superstition—bending spoons, aliens who play doctor on abducted people, weeping statues, and chummy angels.

These things are brain dust, nothing more. We're a foolish animal, making devils and fairies from our fears and desires. And yet . . . yesterday he thought that he heard a child's footsteps running across the bedroom floor upstairs. It must simply have been the wind in the trees, but hairs rose on the back of his neck. Later, lying in bed, he had heard voices in the attic, and this morning, preparing to shave, his face seemed unfamiliar, something puffy like dough.

Pushing aside his coffee mug and pill bottles, he reaches for the stack of student essays that has rested fallow for a week. He is only a part-time teacher now, having chucked his position at Tulane three years ago to live in Duluth, where Sandy, also freshly adrift from a belly-up marriage, had children in high school. The girl has taken her sprinkle of freckles to Grinnell College in Iowa, and the boy now prunes his trial beard at Carleton College in southern Minnesota. Blake had known Sandy for a few years before their marriage and was always amazed at the time she spent on her children—the swim meets, the music lessons, the trips to the library or the museum. Now her kids are gone.

His own son is gone too, but differently. Ralph did not attended college, and Blake warned him that he would end up out in the cold. Blake recalls the night—actually it had been 4:00 am—when he found Ralph passed out on the sidewalk by the house in New Orleans.

"You're buying yourself a ticket to a lonely town," Blake warned, steering Ralph up the steps and into the vestibule.

A week later, perhaps for spite, Ralph tossed his duffel bag in his old Honda and headed for Canada. Blake stood on the porch waving goodbye, his arms performing the heart's disabled semaphore, and later that day he wept among the objects left behind in Ralph's room—an aquarium, an old computer—wondering how he had let himself fail his son in his boyhood.

Now he remembers isolated moments of Ralph's childhood, moments that grow vague and turn to smoke at either end—the lost dog, the time Ralph broke his leg in high school football, the girl Ralph took to the prom, a dark-eyed Cajun with a voice as soft as moonlight. Blake had never communicated much with Ralph, and Ralph's last two phone calls have been at least five months apart. Maybe if they had gone to more Saints games, more fishing trips, more . . . .

The fall quarter at UMD is nearly over, and the papers are the last from his introduction to literature class. Barry Blaine's effort is on top of the stack. When he started teaching during graduate school in Houston in the Sixties, Blake connected with his students naturally, as allies who shared a world view. He had known what his students were majoring in and where they thought they were headed in life. But after he moved to New Orleans and as the age difference increased, the students' apathy seemed to grow, and he became like someone standing on the shore talking to a receding ship. Now he no longer cares about his students' personal goals. Even in his glory days at Tulane, few of his undergraduates were ever really influenced by the literature that he taught, and all too many barely concealed their contempt before drifting off into law firms, corporations, and marriages—wherever it is they go.

Blake made his name outside of the classroom, writing elaborately documented books on Faulkner, Hemingway, and Fitzgerald, and then, when "theory" was the happening thing, writing a witty and intricate performance for the cognoscenti on the topic of semiotics and interpretation. His semesters were punctuated with airplane flights to conferences to promote his ideas by day and to cultivate the usual gentrified dissipations by night. Along the way, the humanizing influence of literature that he had believed in so strongly—the liberalizing power of the great texts that Northrop Frye had written of so eloquently—turned first into a marketable piety, then a polite fiction, and finally an antiquated formula.

Barry Blaine's attitude toward literature is one of dull contempt, although not the contempt born of familiarity. Blake rests his hand on Blaine's page and a half, recalling all of the dissertations he has read and rubber-stamped by graduate students of various sexes: slender young men doing Whitman or Auden, macho types working on Hemingway, and nervous, nicotine-stained women in their smoky attics madly interpreting writers of what Blake calls the Ophelia School—Woolf, Plath, Sexton, and the other lady suicides. Blake sighs, glances out the window again at the child bobbing about beyond the snowdrift, the child in his "lamb-white days." Blake takes up Blaine's paper, which begins:

> *I don't care if Fitzgerald is from Minnesota, I think this story "Winter Dreams" which is only made up anyway is stupid. Why should this main character be smitten to hear that this golf course snob got old and ugly and wasn't exactly the bell of the ball anymore? Like, doesn't everyone. What he should do is forget about her and get on with his life. And since you told us to compare the story to the relevance of our own life; I'll say right here that I certainly don't intend to go through life pulling a bunch of baggage from my supposedly good old college days in Duluth. In the three body paragraphs of this essay I will prove three main reasons why Fitzgerald's "hero" is stupid.*

Blake tries to imagine Barry's future, visualizing only a stream of pizzas and beer bottles vanishing over the horizon. Like Ralph, Barry is squandering his best years, positioning himself on the outside. Blake marks the essay for grammar and spelling, tossing a red loop around "bell" and adding the truant question mark. He catches himself thinking that he has been telling Barry about the semicolon for the past thirty years. But he writes instead that the paper is a half-hearted effort and scribbles a C at the bottom.

He sets the pen aside and recalls the many "made up" characters that his freshman have met this quarter—the scrivener staring at the wall, the young man succumbing to despair in a New England forest, the failed writer dying of gangrene in Africa, the woman at her ironing board telling of her daughter's misplaced childhood, the black teacher who can't save his brother from drugs, the man struggling to build a fire in the Artic winter, the scabrous old angel with enormous wings. So many stories. So many worlds.

"So many stories," he says to the air.

But these storied lives float increasingly on the borders of Blake's consciousness, which these past weeks has been steadily detaching itself from his career, from his former life, and from old ideals that have grown vague like snow drifting far away in a town to which he won't return. The stories he has just finished teaching are as peripheral now to the chiaroscuro of his own made-up life as they are to his students' made-up lives. Because everyone's life is invented, lived with the aid of the delete key and the cut-and-paste. Our storied lives.

On the radio, *Morning Edition* is over, and now motes dance in the air by the window as Branford Marsalis plays Faure's *Pavane*. Outside the wind has lessened, and the child in his red cap continues to toss about in the same place by the alley, perhaps more slowly as though he too is moving to the pavane. The scene has been further altered by vehicles and pedestrians, although there are still a few snow-draped cars parked on the street, waiting like forlorn sheep. Further down the street a golden retriever bursts from a back door, seemingly propelled by its whirling tail, and plunges into the show, gleefully bucking its way here and there in the yard. Blake turns again to the papers, grading three in a single effort of concentration, circling misspellings and occasionally observing that a sentence is garbled or that an assertion needs support.

The scream of the telephone gives him a start that subsides into a wash of worry. Maybe it's Ralph again. The conversation yesterday hadn't gone well, with Ralph garbled and drunk . . . or something. Ralph had moved back to New Orleans after his flight to Canada, but yesterday he had claimed to be in Minot. What, Blake wondered, would make a young man from New Orleans end up in North Dakota? But this question was drowned by Blake's suspicion that the money he seemed to plead for would be traded for whatever it is that they snort or pop these days. Nothing was clear, but there had also been something about someone named Jenny.

It isn't that Blake lacks funds. On the contrary, he played the academic game at Tulane as smoothly as Marsalis plays the sax, schmoozing where schmoozing was needed, earning royalties on his textbook, and becoming the highly visible and stipended head of an institute on cultural theory. He invested fortunately, and ultimately received a plump inheritance when his mother cashed in her mortal coil. In the final years in New Orleans, he measured time with a Rolex and spanned the distances to Commander's Palace or the Rex Ball in a red Jaguar.

But after Blake's divorce, Ralph stumbled up against the law one spaced-out night in the French Quarter and was in and out of rehab programs until the night that Blake hauled him off of the sidewalk. Then Ralph lit out for points north. Early on in his New Orleans years, Blake had navigated his own period of dissipation, hitting the bars until all hours with Hugh Talbot, an ex-peacenik from Los Angeles who was in the process of washing out of Tulane's History Department. He remembers Hugh, gazing into the smoky nights with dirty brown eyes like pennies found in a vacant lot. But Blake pulled his act together, and now he insists that he won't finance the blowing of his son's circuits.

As he stands and turns toward the phone, rehearsing his lecture on self-destruction, a form glides again into the basement stairway like stage mist drifting into the wings, or a presentiment slipping back into some cellar of the mind. It occurs to him that Ralph became a sort of glider, slipping out of sight while Blake revved his Jag and polished his prose. And Blake himself had drifted away from Ralph's mother in those years when pretty and pliant graduate students—usually not those of the Ophelia School—were a chain of available daisies. We are all gliders, he thinks, slipping off into the outlands of one another's lives, existing always in the subjunctive, the sum of shifting configurations, like the history of a cloud before it disintegrates.

But it's Sandy on the phone, not Ralph, calling from her hotel room in Minneapolis. Her father's condition is unchanged, and the doctors say he could hang on for two or three weeks. She'll be home later today to wait it out in Duluth, and for an instant Blake pictures her car making the final, swooping drop down I 35 toward Duluth and the lake. Sandy is not welcome at her sister's house in Minneapolis, and there is no point in donating hundreds to the Hyatt. Sandy is a no-nonsense person, cool and efficient, seldom emotional. Considering the long-established foolishness of her sister, it had probably been right for Sandy to insist on the power of attorney when her father's mind began its glide elsewhere.

But Blake wonders if she could have been more considerate of the others' feelings, if she isn't a tad too impatient with the normal back-and-forth of human relationships. The negotiation over the power of attorney had not been a pleasant episode—an obscene squabble, really, conducted by an open grave. Deep within himself, where not even Blake will see clearly, something he'd rather not know about Sandy stirs. But at moments these recent weeks he has felt that, as a frightened person might glance down a cellar stair, avoiding the recesses and the shadows, much of his life has been lived looking the other way.

The child across the street is motionless behind the snowdrift, and it's odd that he has played in one spot for the past forty-five minutes on a cold morning. The radio had said twenty degrees. Then it dawns on Blake. Perhaps the child hasn't been playing. Perhaps he has been stuck in the snowdrift, struggling to free himself. It happened to a kid Blake had known in Iowa, a kid who froze to death. If this child is trapped in the snow, then his stillness now could mean . . . .

Blake doesn't know the parents' names, not to mention their phone number, and the police could take half an hour to arrive. His throat is dry and inflamed and he's dizzy when he stands, but he must go out. He struggles into a jacket in the front entry, not wasting time to tug on boots. As he closes the outside door behind him, he hears the phone ring. The snowdrift over his sidewalk is nearly to his knees. He plunges around the corner of the house and then across the street, stumbling and high-stepping, clutching his collar about his neck, dreading what the coming moments might reveal. But as he approaches the snowdrift, things change.

"Jesus Christ," he says to no one.

It isn't a child at all, and Blake realizes that the stake with the red flag, all but hidden now by the snowdrift, had been there all autumn long, marking the corner of a garden where, perhaps, some landscaping had been intended. What had made him think that the flag was the capped head of a little boy, and that his own footprints would document a heroic effort rather than an old man's folly? What sort of stupid drama had he, by way of misinterpretation, written into the wind and snow?

Without overshoes, gloves, or cap, each frozen breath slicing down his throat like a knife and his nose flooding onto his lips, Blake is a miserable child himself. The winds leap from trees and careen down the alley, brawling, and clouds darken the air. Swirling snow hisses from the branches of a pine, and as he turns away from the misread scene another ghostly observer glides away into its twilight world. He wipes his nose on his sleeve and stamps his numbing feet, absurdly reluctant to begin the battle back through the snow to Sandra's house, which is dark and empty and seems somehow to be sliding to a great distance beyond the street and up the hillside, as though not merely the universe but the earth itself were an expanding ball of ice. Blake realizes that he has probably locked himself out and that, in any case, the phone has stopped ringing.

Leaving Jenny

Rest Stop

I'm trying to get to Minot, but when I pulled into this pit stop south of Duluth it was raining and I switched the engine off. Force of habit. I bought the Cutlass Ciera for Jenny two years ago. It had some rust so the price was good, but it never starts after the rain. *It's chillin'*, Jenny says. Maybe the plugs get wet, or a wire. I'm not a mechanic. But you don't want to leave your engine running while you're taking a whiz. You don't want to find your car gone. Jenny says I do stupid things, but I say they're only careless things. It's that my mind is somewhere else. Like Minot.

Maybe I 35 to Duluth isn't the best route from Des Moines. I didn't check a road map. I figured I'd just drive to Duluth, then head west. They got a town up there called Bemidji that's probably on the way. Then I'll go through Fargo. Or is it Grand Forks? I've never been to North Dakota.

The rain is finished. I'm camped on top of this picnic table getting some air. Way up, a vee of ducks moves slow like they're swimming in tar. I was finding animal shapes in the clouds, but then I remembered not to imagine things. It's a promise I made to myself. I should prop up the hood of the Cutlass with the baseball bat, find the rag under the seat, and pat the plugs and wires down. But it's no big deal. It's not like I haven't spent the night in a rest area before.

Instead of opening the hood, I've been thinking about that truck stop down by Minneapolis. There was this blond waitress with big tits behind the counter. She wore a pink uniform with a name tag that said Mabel. Her hair was pinned up, but some of it fell forward and she kept brushing it back. She kept tapping her pencil on her little note pad. I thought waitresses were only named Mabel in old movies, but sometimes I think that my whole life is an old movie, an old black and white. So I asked her how much it would be to get a bed for a couple of hours. It was only three in the afternoon, but I wanted to lie down and I'd never slept at a truck stop before. She said the beds are for truckers only, which I knew. I thought I'd ask anyway.

It's after six, but up here it stays light pretty late. I figure the car will start before dark. Before the daylight leaks away like a tire going flat. I figure I can make it to Duluth and find a motel. Then I'll go to Minot tomorrow.

The rest area has a scenic overlook with a sign that tells you about the scene. The sign is about drainage. It says that this part of the country is odd because rainwater will drain in any direction. There's a north/south divide and an east/west divide, like the top of a pyramid. Rain falling here can end up in the Atlantic Ocean, in the Gulf of Mexico, in Hudson Bay, and so on. You can tell from the sign that they're kind of proud of it up here. It's a real special deal, geographically speaking.

I'm hunched on a picnic table above the scenery like that statue of the man thinking, except I'm eating an Almond Joy. There's a telephone next to the candy machine in the building, and I could slide off this picnic table and call Jenny. It would be simple. Me and Jenny have been together off and on for six or seven years, maybe eight counting the two I spent in the joint for helping her batshit brother navigate a load of weed across the Gulf of Mexico. He wanted to make a mark in the weed business, like it's baseball or some art form. I don't know jack about boats and I can't swim, but I figured what the hell.

So me and Jenny go way back, and maybe we can work it out.

That's what I'll say if I call. I'll say that I can turn around and get to the trailer park by midnight and she can have her Cutlass back. But I won't call. There'd be too much that I'd have to stare in the face.

Sometimes Jenny sobers up and wears her best clothes. She bags the empties and makes plans. It's nice at first, but if you look close, it isn't the real Jenny. It's Jenny's fantasy of Jenny—her longed-for Jenny, who drifts away in a day or two like a cloud. I say that these cleaned-up days never last and that dreams aren't the same as plans. Then she yells at me for going down that road. She says I'm full of dark roads. It's too much work thinking about Jenny and her issues. Everyone says issues now, even when it's just an old-fashioned jumble of drunkenness and deceit. Not that I didn't drink too. We drank some, me and Jenny.

So I won't call. As far as Jenny is concerned, I've vanished without a trace. A missing person. I'll go to Minot. I don't know what they do in Minot or if they have issues or go way back. I'm not interested. I want to get a room and go to the diner in the morning for pancakes and in the evening for a burger with fries. I'll go to movies and maybe go fishing. I hope you can fish around Minot, but beyond that I don't care. I don't want to meet anyone. If you can't fish, it's no big deal.

There's a breeze, and branches click in the trees like latches. The clouds have clawed their way off toward Wisconsin, and pretty soon I'll walk down the hill, get the rag and the bat, lift the hood, and pat things down. Maybe I'll toss out the can that's been rolling around under the seat and scoop out the candy wrappers. If the car starts I'll drive to Duluth. I won't call anyone in Duluth either, and tomorrow I'll go to Minot, after driving through Grand Forks, or maybe Fargo.

Going Home

On most days Pete understands that he shouldn't drive, but this morning he fussed when Kathy swept the keys from the kitchen counter and into the pocket of her old plaid jacket. *We're not going to drift into old age having killed some poor child in one of Pete's moments*, Kathy had said to Pastor Seabold three weeks ago, when she went to him about Pete's changes. Kathy thanked God that Pete, after all the years of playing the boss, was compliant when she put her foot down.

So it had been a nice morning, the county roads disappearing behind groves of trees or drifting away forever into fields, while the car on the main highway glided and turned like a swallow among farms and around the west end of Lake Winona, still lovely under a sunny sky even though the trees had shed their autumn colors. And the nice morning became a nostalgic one in Glenn Oaks, where Pete and Kathy had met as teachers and where the kids had been born.

Their old schoolhouse, where Ronnie and Jenny started grade school before the move to Des Moines, was renovated now and housed a yarn shop, a pottery studio, a Vietnamese restaurant called Taste of Saigon, and other small businesses working the precincts of pleasure rather than necessity—a good place to dawdle some time away. But it was strange to see this little corner of Glenn Oaks, a no-nonsense agricultural town in the old days, trying to be a miniature tourist destination out here among the corn fields and hog farms.

During the lunch of spring rolls and chicken with lemon grass, Pete remarked that it isn't roast beef and mashed potatoes anymore. He had been in Saigon during the war as a supply clerk, and now he was having Vietnamese food in his home town in Iowa. It was something strange that he tried to think about.

"Everything's different," Pete said, idly examining an unused chopstick before returning to his fork. A few months ago it would have been an angry remark, and Kathy was grateful to Dr. Clough, despite misgivings about how medicine has replaced prayer in our modern world.

"Yes," she replied, saddened to look at his eyes, vague as clouds. "Things are different now. But I think it's nice what they've done with the building, don't you?"

Unlocking the Honda after lunch, Kathy looked back to see Pete standing in the parking lane cut into what had been the front yard of Cheryl Mason Elementary and Middle School. Gazing at the trees in the park across the street, hands stuffed in pockets, Pete was listening to music coming from speakers bolted to the school beneath classroom windows. The music was mysterious and calming—played, it seemed, on flute and guitar—and for a moment after it ended Pete's mind remained in the place the music had created.

"That was pretty," he said, shifting his eyes to Kathy. "I wonder if one of the students knows its name."

Students. In these moments of panic, frequent visitors now, Kathy summoned to mind Reverend Seabold's words. *If things get difficult, Kathryn, we'll be there, and God will be there. We're a community. In the meantime, take things a day at a time.*

"It sounded like 'White Christmas' to me. But," she added quickly, "we could go back and ask. Someone in one of the shops must be in charge of the music they pipe out."

Pete knew that the kids start Christmas music before Thanksgiving these days, but it hadn't been "White Christmas" coming from the school, he was sure of that. Kathy hadn't been listening. Ever since his sessions with Dr. Clough, Pete had become a good listener. Pete had gone to Dr. Clough five months ago. *Think my head's a little on the fritz, Doc,* he had said, trying to be jaunty. The doctor recommended music along with the pills, Seroquel and Aricept, and now Pete loved music that he had ignored all of his life. And the other day, with Kathy at his side in the Barnes & Noble in Des Moines, he had bought two CDs that Frank—Dr. Clough—had suggested, a classical guitar collection by Sharon Isbin and some piano music by Bill Evans.

Later that afternoon, sitting by the window in his study, he had listened to Evans play "Some Other Time," the low notes tolling like a distant bell and the melody notes falling like raindrops on stone. And looking out into the backyard at the place by the lilac where Jenny's playhouse had been, he sobbed to remember the time, so long ago, when she had stood on a corner in the rain after a Saturday movie. Pete, sitting in that same room, his mind occupied with matters of inventory and taxes, had forgotten to come for her.

Inside the front door, by the entrance to Taste of Saigon, Pete stopped a young girl, a pretty girl except for the BB stuck to the side of her nose.

"What's the name of that song?"

The girl's look was cute and quizzical, with wrinkling brows and a tip of the head.

"We'd like to find out about the music that they pipe outside," Kathy explained. "Do you know who's in charge of that?"

The girl smiled, saying that the lady in the gift shop on the third floor handled the music system. Ignoring the new elevator, Pete hunched his shoulders and trudged up the old stairway with its terrazzo steps, steps, Kathy thought, that scurrying feet had worn to the shape of the upturned palms of angels. The Angels' Ladder, she had called the stairs back in her teaching days.

"I taught English in a room where that gift shop is now. Do you remember that, Pete? And your math class . . . ." She had spoken to him earlier about their old classrooms and the new layout of the building, but Pete had not paid attention. Now he receded in front of her around a turn, and her voice trailed into silence.

Later, before the drive home, they crossed the street to a picnic table in the park, stirring the leaves as they walked. Kathy buttoned her red plaid jacket. In a few weeks, perhaps days, it would be winter. It was sunny in Glenn Oaks today, though, and despite all the changes, Glenn Oaks was still home.

But Pete was irritated that the lady in the gift shop had said that it was just a Christmas song performed by a local pianist who had "burned" his own CD, whatever that meant. The music had been new and strange, something never heard before. When he protested, the lady had glanced at Kathy and said that perhaps her helper had put something else on while she was out of the shop.

Now, looking across the park to the small, rainbow-colored village of children's swings and slides and climbing stations, Pete tried to let his anger wash away. *Imagine warm rain washing all over your body, washing it all away*, Dr. Frank—no, Dr. Clough—had advised.

"Ronnie likes to play there," Pete said.

Pete had never been attractive. But Kathy herself was rather short and wide, and she had learned at an early age to resist the culture's celebration of appearance. Moreover, Christianity calls on us to rise above such things. But now the carelessness of Pete's appearance saddened her. Perched on top of the picnic table, his old tan jacket unzipped and his pants tugged up above his ankles, Pete seemed vulnerable—a small, round figurine rocking like a ball about to roll off onto the ground.

"Ronnie and Jenny both used to play here, Pete. But all this plastic-looking stuff is new. Remember how it used to be a row of swings, the aluminum slide, and that old push-around that tilted so? And the path worn so deep in the ground from all the kids running along side, pushing and jumping on? And sometimes Ronnie and Jenny would come here and play in the grass in the evening until the stars came out. Do you remember?"

It was always Ronnie, Kathy thought. When, at the age of sixteen, Ronnie snuck home one night decorated with snakes and daggers, Pete sang the praises of tattoos, of ink poked into the flesh in dingy salons. And when Ronnie landed in jail, Pete raged at a system run by *goons and Nazis* who jail a boy for bringing some marijuana home from vacation. He wrote letters to senators and even flew to Baton Rouge, where he tried to force his way into the office of Governor Edwin Edwards, shouting to the guards who restrained him *that Edwards is the ___ who belongs in jail.*

Pete had always minimized Ronnie's mistakes. At the same time, at least until the pills, Pete had spent his days complaining about government, about journalists, about the neighbors—maybe his defense of Ronnie was tied in with his general antagonism to the world. *We're a community*, Reverend Seabold had said, and

Kathy often wondered what their lives would have been if Pete had lived with a stronger sense of community. If it hadn't always been us against them.

Now Jenny's life was in the commode, and the worst that she had done was to breeze in from New Orleans with that same bum who talked Ronnie into so much trouble. It drove Pete into rages—*that ghoul is feeding on our children*, he said. But unlike Ronnie, Jenny had telephoned nearly once a month after she moved away—and Jenny sent Christmas cards. Ronnie had scribbled one letter from prison, incoherent words strung out carelessly like shorts and socks on a clothesline, which Pete treasured like The Constitution. At the same time, it had been as though Jenny didn't exist. It was an inexplicable prejudice and the biggest disappointment of Kathy's marriage.

And yet maybe Kathy was mistaken. If Pete really didn't care about Jenny, why all the attempts to tell her that she was throwing her life away on a drunk and a criminal, on a man who had ruined her brother? Was it that Pete really loved Jenny, or was it that Pete was sick—was it that Jenny's bum had appeared at the right moment to be the lightning rod for anger that really boiled up from the chemistry in Pete's head? Dr. Clough had said that brain chemistry was the culprit. And then Kathy despaired at her inability to distinguish love from chemistry.

Ronnie disappeared. Kathy pictures him walking through the prison gate, looking around in the sunlight, and then dissolving as in a movie. There had been no phone call, no letter. Nothing. Kathy and Pete didn't know if he was still alive. But now it was time to take care of Jenny, who was drinking again and had lost her job after that drifter stole her car. Kathy had tried to bring Jenny to church for counseling, but instead Jenny talked about going to California. *Everything loose ends up in California*, Pete had said. Kathy replied that with money to back her up, she could sit down with Jenny to explore alternatives and make plans. Maybe she and Jenny could open the small dress shop that they had always talked about when Jenny was young. But to be more than just pipe dreams, alternatives require money. Pete agreed to sign over the thousands that had grown and then dwindled in a Vanguard mutual fund. *I will. . .*, he said, his voice rising and drifting off like smoke caught in a breeze. But nothing had happened.

Kathy watched a golden retriever, fresh off the leash, race about, pulled this way and that by the needs of his nose. Off by the sidewalk, its owner pressed a cell phone to his head. The retriever stopped near the picnic table and began to circle as though trying to twist itself into the ground. When it stopped and hunched its back, Kathy looked away.

"Fortune cookies," Pete said. Kathy did not know if it was an obscure comment about the dog at its business.

"What about them, dear? Did you read your fortune?"

She knew that he had not. Pete used to laugh at people who even pretended, just for fun, that there is something like fate or destiny. And she remembered, almost like it was yesterday and not twenty years ago or more, how he had laughed at Jenny the time, saying *please, please* in the cutest way, she had wanted to have her fortune told at the county fair. *Our lives are what we make them*, he had asserted so often during their marriage, even when life was becoming anything but what they had planned. In The Taste of Saigon, the cookies had rested untouched on the plastic tray.

"Sorry about that." It was the dog's owner, a young man in jogging clothes. Slipping the cell phone into a pocket and producing a plastic bag from another, he stooped to clean up after his dog. Kathy smiled, but Pete, still rocking like a ball, was lost in a jumble of partial thoughts that, as Kathy imagined it, form and disappear like soap bubbles in the tub.

It had occurred to Pete that the cookies had been wrong, that they hadn't had fortune cookies in Saigon during the war. They were probably just a childish little pleasure that Americans expect, some gesture toward a myth of a mysterious Orient. But it would be too much effort to say that, to find the words, and the thought was already drifting away like smoke in the trees. Kathy turned up the collar of her jacket against a freshening breeze and followed Pete's gaze past the trees to the shops that lined Maple Street.

"Maple Street used to turn into the dirt road that ran down to Frenchman's Creek," she said. "It was so nice walking along the path by the creek, don't you think? We enjoyed it so, and Jenny did too! It's where Jenny found that dog, Rusty, that we had until the neighbor boy's car hit him. We could drive down there before we start back. Would you like that?"

Sometimes, when Kathy thought about the early days of their marriage, days when the future shimmered down a curving road beyond sun-drenched fields, yearning swelled like a physical thing in the small of her back. For a moment she was twenty-two again, and the longing for a bright tomorrow was absolutely real. But these moments had become increasingly rare, as though, paradoxically, desire had been dulled by its own repetition. It was like the longing expressed in "White Christmas," except of course the song was about the past—but no, it was about the future too. Kathy wondered at Pete's ability—because it *was* an ability, nearly—to hear the song as something lovely and new after all these years. The moment passed, and she was left with a fear that now Frenchman's Creek might be a neglected, littered place of broken glass, cast-off wrappers, and worse—a place for addicts and derelicts.

"Some other time," he said, not sure whether he was merely repeating the name of the Bill Evans piece. The song and his own thoughts mingled oddly, one dissolving into the other. For a moment blurred images of the lilac tree and Jenny's playhouse tried to form in his mind. But they drifted and faded, and his eyes moved to the sky. High above, a ragged formation of ducks pushed southward as a train whistle threw its arch of sound across the fields and the creek.

Then, finding Kathy beside him on the picnic table, Pete tried to remember what it was that they had come here to do.

Aftertimes

The sideboards of houses, trash in the streets, relationships—everything rots fast in New Orleans. Everything turns to mush. When I lived there with Jenny—this was a long time ago—our bar was Les Bons Temps Roulez on Magazine Street, which was right across from our rented shotgun. A shotgun is a narrow house that goes straight back, one room behind the other. You slept in the back, had breakfast in the middle, and walked out the front. The roof sagged in the middle like a hammock, and the porch had a hole where a foot had gone through. Lee Harvey Oswald had lived on our block, but that was before our time.

On the good evenings we'd step out the front door together, avoid the hole, and walk down the four decomposing steps, the hot summer air wrapping itself around you like wet towels. We'd wait for a car or two to pass, and then we'd be shooting pool or shooting the shit with Ned, who owned the Bons Temps. There was a room in back with a great juke where Jenny taught me to dance. I loved the strut and glide of the tango, and I loved holding Jenny during the slow parts as the violin and the bandoneon yearned.

Sometimes Ned would have boiled crawfish. We'd sit by the window in the glow of the neon sign, breaking off the heads and pealing the shells, me with a Bud and Jenny sipping a Turbo Dog. She'd suck the juices out of the heads like a Cajun, laughing when I pretended to puke. And we'd talk about the sailors and whores in the bars of Buenos Aires over a hundred years ago, when the tango was born. Jenny's thoughts flared like matches in the dim room, and we'd try to imagine those lives, the violence and longing of the men on shore from their ships and of the women in the dark brothels. Jenny said that abandoned things have their own special beauty.

On bad evenings, or afternoons, Jenny would stumble down the steps alone, yelling over her shoulder that she didn't want to see me at the Bons Temps or anywhere else. We had our separate bars for those times. Even on the bad days I desired Jenny. Love is fire. It churned inside of me, but I won't try to describe it. I hate poetry. With Jenny off on one of her tears, I'd sit on the porch and watch the pigeons scavenging in the gutter as the evening gathered in pools between buildings and crept up the storefronts along Magazine. I'd see the lights come on in windows down the block, and I'd shiver to think about how time comes at you from around a corner with a knife in its hand.

Eventually, with everything adrift in night, I'd wander off to find a quiet bar. And often, hours later, I'd lie in a strange bed under a strange roof and watch the darkness leak away, leaving the dawn behind like something drowned. The next day we'd find our separate ways back to the shotgun, Jenny and me, usually to sleep some more, sometimes, with a blade of early light slicing through trees and under the drawn shades, to sit quietly in the kitchen and sip tea, to say a few words—*you okay? yeah, I'll survive*—a few words drifting like dust.

Now and then during these aftertimes Jenny would come from the shower clean and scented, a towel turbaned around her hair, and make plans to patch our lives together. Maybe we'd open a bike store in that empty building down the block, or maybe take courses at Tulane or UNO. What if we went to visit her folks in Des Moines? She thought that maybe her daddy would help us land on our feet. That was her phrase—land on our feet, like the drinking life was a circus act. Sometimes the new Jenny, and the new me too, sometimes these new people would last a few days. All the empties would be bagged and gone, the ashtrays wiped and put away, and the smell of cigarettes washed from our hair and clothes.

And during these times we'd drift into an odd sort of backward yearning. Instead of imagining the future the way others do, we invented a fictional past where we had always known each other. We dreamed up a small town and said that we had grown up in it. We talked about the smell of lilacs in the spring and of burning leaves in the long-ago autumns of this imagined town. There was always a mother leaning in a kitchen door, her hair catching the summer sun, always a father trimming a hedge or washing a car. We avoided worms on the sidewalk in the morning after rain and caught grasshoppers during sunny afternoons. There were fireflies in the backyard in the quiet evenings of early summer, when we'd play in the grass until the subsiding light coaxed the stars out one by one. Sitting on the front steps of the shotgun in New Orleans, we pretended to remember the old dirt road by the river and the lost dog we found there one day. Jenny described the train that ran through the valley, its whistle making a lonesome sound.

Maybe we went to Iowa to look for our imagined town. I don't know. It was Jenny's plan and I didn't care. In that long drive up I 55 through Mississippi, Arkansas and Missouri, we drank iced tea from a thermos, ate sandwiches that Jenny had bundled in Saran Wrap, and listened to country-western on the radio. We thought that we knew where we were going. The timing belt broke in West Memphis, where dust devils spiraled in the August heat. Jenny said that West Memphis was a purgatory that we had to pass through to find a new life.

I guess we'd bought into some kind of heartland mythology, but we found that things rot in Iowa too. Jenny's father, Pete, had a black belt in resentment, and her mom, Kathryn, was batty with religion and disappointment. Pete was short, but wide as a door. He'd come at you with a face like a headlight, and he kept a shotgun under the sofa. His neighborhood grocery had been run out of business by the supermarkets. Whenever he cornered someone he'd regurgitate his stump speech in a voice caked with sludge, a speech about how *the fuckers are out to kill ya*.

And just as certainly Kathryn, looming in the background, would come back with something about *trust in the Lord*. They had their separate tools for simplifying, for scraping the messiness from life, and their eternal back-and-forth was held together by a small annuity. I don't know how we could have thought they'd do us any good, how we could have thought that it was a plan when it was only like one of those shapes you pretend to see in the clouds in order to pass the time. It was a long time ago, and we were stupid.

We got a beat-up trailer and found a trailer park on the edge of Des Moines. We called it Sullen Acres. At night I'd dream of wings and bright eyes moving away in a rush through the trees. Jenny wore an orange uniform and served hash browns and eggs in a truck stop. She gained weight, and her ankles began to swell like her mother's.

I tended bar at a tumble-down redneck hang on the county road and spent two days in jail after waving the .38 in Pete's glaring face. He had blown in ranting about me and Jenny, and I responded that I loved her. *Speak English!* he screamed. *You're destroying her life!* He swung a bar stool and hit Willy Martin, who was at the bar minding his own business. Willy dropped like empty clothes, and I reached for the pistol. Kathryn drooped behind him in the smoke, surrounded by grinning good-ol'-boys, her hair collapsed around her head like a dead bird. I suppose she was muttering something about acting "nice," her favorite word. But maybe Pete was right. Our tango days had skulked away, and sunrise was always a slap in the face.

Once, toward the end, Jenny sat me down in the trailer among empty chili cans and greasy dishes to make plans, as she had in New Orleans, brushing her hair back in a businesslike way and tapping a pencil on a small spiral notebook, straining to push some of the old brightness into her voice, the old springtime into her eyes. *We have to make something of our lives,* she said. *It won't just happen like from destiny or something.* My hand was in a cast from a fight, and after a long night I felt like hammered shit. All I could say was, *Yeah, right.* She stormed out, but later I found her, quiet as evening, wandering down the road. When I asked how things were, she shrugged and said, *Life is only another form of weather.* It's true that Jenny was like weather, like wind that tears itself apart until it's only scraps of wind here and there.

And it's true that the notion to leave Jenny blew in like a front. And I didn't know where I was heading, climbing into her rusty

Oldsmobile that dragged-out morning when she finally came home to sleep after a four-day blowout. She had been sober for a month, but after the planning session fizzled I guess that she thought it was time to bust loose. Jenny was punctual about her blowouts, punctual as winter. I was eighty miles up the interstate before I thought to park my butt here in Minot.

It's barren here, and the wind hits hard. It's been six years. I met a girl who likes to fish. She's pregnant now, and we might get married. But it's nothing special. I wonder if Jenny thinks about me, and about how I took her car. It was probably a story she told for a few months. I was probably a character in a story that stopped being told.

Dreams glimmer away, and time waits by the road with a knife. Our lives are not intended things. We had dreamed, Jenny and me, that in Iowa we'd live at the edge of a quiet town and raise horses. We'd have a place like one that we had seen from the car window, speeding by on the highway, a house with a solid roof and a yard with cedars and a maple tree. There would a pond reflecting clouds and sky, and a dog.

Looking out from our porch in the late afternoon, we'd see far away an abandoned barn sinking into the rippling grass like a battered ship. We'd sip tea on our porch and talk about Buenos Aires, about the sailors and the tango and about going there one day. Maybe, as we daydream on our porch, a hawk high up arcs with bowed wings like it's following curves in the sky itself. Then, as the evening climbs the hills and the trees exhale insects, the grass and barn and hawk dissolve in a gray wash. And I still see in my imagination the road that passes our longed-for place, leading away as darkness gathers.

Pablo and I

I met Pablo Neruda in the Minneapolis Public Library two summers ago, shortly after my wife's apostasy. Crystal was very *a la mode*, assuring me that I was "okay" and that I mustn't feel "inadequate." It was just that she needed to "move on"—there were drinks to mix, beaches to prowl. Whatever.

She left with Frank, who, twice a year for over a decade, had shoved his little mirror around in our respective mouths with rubber-gloved fingers. I've imagined him planting his pick in my molars while plotting his flight with Crystal. Because women are the weaker sex, it should be no surprise when the wifely eye wanders. But Frank? Our dentist? It was an ego slam. I am, in point of fact, a man of wit and classical good looks, but there were some rough nights of Coors and self scrutiny amidst the babble of jazz and amplified poetry that constituted the nightly fare at *Sylvia's*.

I thought about new interests once the happy adulterers were airborne. Skydiving? A scuba club? The occult? What finally felt best, less desperate and more authentically me, was to return to the research that I had begun for my dissertation thirty years earlier but had abandoned during the ennui of the Seventies. It concerned the communication systems employed by plant life—how the lilacs and the petunias share information about the people who plant them and the animals that prowl among them. I had defined a vocabulary and syntax of smells and had begun work on the process by which plants communicate through chemical changes that they create in the soil. Of course I kept my day job of peddling information in the business community, and my vego-linguistic research was a sideline.

I was into some exciting stuff about the chemistry of dirt when I first noticed Pablo, who occupied the body of an ordinary bag lady named Linda. Not coincidentally, it was also the day that I first spotted the culture police questioning the lady at the checkout desk of the library. In their blue suits and red ties, they interrupted their interrogation from time to time to mutter into pocket-sized recorders.

On the one hand, I was concerned for Linda, since her interest in the nineteenth-century anarchists—I had heard her voice it only moments before to a librarian—could arouse suspicion. On the other hand, I believed that well-meaning people should adjust their concerns and tastes with patriotism and the war on terrorism in mind. I, for instance, had adopted the punitive policy of no longer wearing my camelhair jacket. But I was also aware of our government's prohibitions against various kinds of biological research, and perhaps my botanical studies were in the cross hairs. In any case, the cops showed no overt interest in the slovenly Linda—nor in your dapper narrator.

As for Linda's slovenliness, s/he wore the same filthy wrap-around skirt each day and carried a gunny sack containing his "stuff." Age spots flecked his hands like rust. I'd glance up from my stack of reference material to see him—in my mind I called him "old baggy-boobs"—slip as quietly as smoke into a nearby carrel. And sometimes, passing behind him on my way out for air, I'd glance over his shoulder to see in what political tome his mind was bivouacked that day.

Over the weeks, perhaps in response to my poorly disguised attentions, the bag-lady persona slowly morphed. His boobs perked up. His boobs became beautiful bouncing bunnies. One day, as he was reading Ricardo's *Principles of Political Economy*, I detected the scent of a modest but coy perfume. A few days later I noticed that the finger tips that turned the pages of Proudhon's

What Is Property? were manicured and sported a magenta polish. And of course during this time the clothing and hair underwent a similar day-by-day upgrade.

When we finally spoke in the outer hall—I nearly blundered into him as he emerged from the ladies' room shaking water from his hands—his first observation had to do with the oddity of reading.

"You look at these black ink marks on paper," he said, "and suddenly another voice is talking in your head and saying things that you've never dreamed could be said. It is absolutely the strangest thing."

My own head had passed through a decade of intense inner chatter, and it was exciting to meet someone who spoke of such things, even though his voices were pre-recorded on the printed page.

"Donuts?" I replied.

He nodded, and we made straight for Adolph's Donut Emporium on the other side of Nicollet Avenue, which is where Linda told me—having to repeat it twice through a cheekful of Adolph's famous squid-filled éclair—that he was Pablo.

Life is a minefield. You learn that your stock broker, who doubles as your golfing pal, is selling you junk. The dentist who tugs your mouth about and drills your teeth is playing the double-backed beast with your wife, who in turn is planning her great escape as the two of you sip latte at a sidewalk café. One day your neighbor, with whom you've discussed global warming and epidemiology over the back fence, is perp-walked off in handcuffs for molesting Cub Scouts. Life is full of unsightly creatures crawling under the surface, so Linda being Pablo wasn't so bad. Linda being Pablo was, in fact, quite a blast.

Of course I was not so smitten as to forget that Pablo had once entertained a serious jones for the "struggles" of the less refined class. But he had also held important political positions in Chile and, at least toward the end, had kept a rather elaborate and ceremonial household in Valparaiso. I assured myself that a person living with Pablo—*this* Pablo—needn't fear coming home to find him in a state of proletarian regression, dozing, perhaps, in a slew of vomit and cigarette butts.

When Pablo and I left Adolph's, stuffed to our tongue bolts, his hand offered my arm a lingering farewell.

Later that day, I walked back to my apartment whistling little melodies—things from *Cats* and *Les Miz*. I chuckled to the invisible creatures that filled the air around me, and I bounded steps two at a time. The next morning, despite an e-mail from my lawyer concerning a rather nasty lawsuit—nasty lawsuits are the current in which my business swims—I bellowed show tunes and whistled arias while frying eggs. As is often the case, my bellowing was soon accompanied by my neighbor's inept drumming on our adjoining wall. And while I try to sympathize with his musical aspirations, I am always dismayed to find that he has no more rhythm than a rutabaga.

Prompted no doubt by our shared taste for raised-glazed, sugared or fish-filled pastries, Pablo trudged up the hill to my nesting place the following month, a duffle bag slung over a shoulder and a parrot cage dangling from an arm. I lived on a hill south of Loring Park, a park that had developed a tainted reputation as a nocturnal playground for disheveled people of desperate proclivities. But my apartment was three blocks up a winding street, with an imposing Episcopalian Church at the bottom of the hill. I often imagined that the church and the park faced each other like ancient adversaries, although in truth the façade of the church faced slightly away from the park as if in scorn. At any rate, the church served as a buffer between my own life and the dusky goings-on of the park.

On our second evening as roomies, Pablo and I took my spiffy Accord ten blocks south on Nicollet Avenue to *Sylvia's*, an unpretentious little jazz and poetry club. Juan, the babbling bird, was out of sorts and remained in his cage. As we parked the car, I warned Pablo that poetry is taken seriously at *Sylvia's*. In fact, a few months back someone had been stabbed in the parking lot for defending "The Red Wheelbarrow." Although my rational self laughed at such concern for the outmoded culture, something primitive in me was attracted to *Sylvia's*. Moreover, I thought that Pablo might find it a hoot.

We entered just as Len Grazione was finishing a set, and I was struck immediately by the presence of the blue-suited twosome from the library, now huddled like conspirators at a table in the corner. No doubt it is possible for a musical improvisation to contain encoded terroristic instructions, but with Len, despite his refusal to quit smoking Camels, now considered by some government officials as a sign of misplaced sympathies, they were barking up the wrong sand dune.

Len, who plays electric guitar in a ballad style that meanders between Kenny Burrell and Jim Hall, joined us as Pablo and I cozied up to the bar. I introduced Pablo to Len and then to Bullet, the talkative young bartender with an eagle's nest of blond hair. Len ordered his standard gin fizz, while Pablo and I took Coors. Pablo wore a short skirt that became even shorter when he crossed his legs—stunningly tanned and sculpted legs—on the barstool. His cashmere V-neck sweater provided a tasty presentation of his generous cleavage. It took Bullet—under the bartender's bravado, a deeply conventional kid from Iowa—a minute to get used to Pablo being Pablo.

"Shit, man," Len said. "What you gawkin' at like you's at da circus fo' da firs' time?" You could walk into the bar with a talking brick and Len wouldn't look twice.

"So when they reincarnate you," Bullet asked, ignoring Len, "how do they decide who you come back as?"

"Shit," Len muttered again, bewildered at Bullet's ignorance.

"Lemme bum a cigarette there, Len," Pablo asked. "They give you three choices, Bullet. Then they sort of put their heads together and pick the one that fires their jets. Actually, they usually pick the middle one, but don't hold me to it." Pablo leaned toward Len for a light.

"Wait a minute," Bullet protested. "You actually put down

Expensive Broad with Big Knockers as one of your choices? Why, in *Canto general* you wrote all about social justice and the poor people of the world! You went to Spain to fight the Fascists! Garcia Lorca was your pal!"

"Bullet," Len protested. "I's amaze you doan know nothin' 'bout how everthin' change. Pablo here, he jus' keepin' wid da time. An' beside, what you doan know is how Pablo never was no Pablo. Dat jus' some name he pull from a ol' hat so's his parens won' know he writin' poems. Ain' I right, Pablo?"

Pablo nodded politely. "My real name was Ricardo Eliezer Neftali Reyes y Basoalto. You can't blame a girl for jumping that ship."

"This just in, Len: slavery's over with," Bullet said. He was giving a few glasses a quick dip in rinse water. "Save the shuffling-black-guy accent for the tourists."

"Well, okay," Len replied. "I was just trying to stay in touch with my roots."

"I can't imagine why," Bullet sneered. Then, turning to Pablo, he asked, "If the cleaned-up you I'm looking at was one of your choices, how come you were just a bag lady when Alex here first met you?"

"The thing is," Pablo replied, "it's like being born. Everyone who comes back starts at the bottom, and it takes nine months to become what you're going to be. I woke up under a bridge with a dog pissing on me. Now I've been back for eight and a half months, so I'm nearly done."

"Sounds like some dish in the oven," Len remarked. "But what's left to become? You look perfect to my blushing eyes."

In fact I was intrigued too, since this nine-month thing was a wrinkle Pablo hadn't mentioned to me. It was my first premonition that Pablo had not told me all there was to know about his re-appearance, a premonition that was enflamed by my observation that the men in the blue suits were now seated at the bar to my right and were calling for two-story whiskeys. Was I the object of their investigation? Was Pablo?

Pablo took a long drag on his cigarette. “I’m going to be a corporate lawyer,” he affirmed. “Juries are allowing far too much in damage settlements these days. It’s bad for business. I’m going to get the laws changed.”

Perhaps he was only trying to placate the eavesdroppers to my right, hunched sullenly over beer bottles and shot glasses. In any case, as he spoke I saw Pablo as a lethal beauty. From his swirling auburn hair to his well-defined calf, he filled the air with sex as surely as Len’s guitar had filled it with music. And Pablo had brains just in case. I pictured a cocktail party peopled by senators and CEOs, and Pablo moving sinuously among them like a river. But one of the many voices in my head, a barely audible voice, whispered that his freshly enlightened political opinions could be merely a ruse. And a companion voice barked that I was being set up.

Eventually Len went back to his guitar, and Bullet turned toward the end of the bar. A drunk had been growing increasingly loud, and now he was slamming Wallace Stevens. Bullet had his game face on, and in a moment, as Bullet held the door open with one hand and gave a healthy shove with the other, the drunk was history. The Blue Two had evaporated unobserved, and by eleven o’clock Pablo and I were driving back down Nicollet Avenue. Soon I’d be spread like honey and licked into dreamland.

Pablo rose early in those days. By the time I was in the kitchen brewing coffee and toasting bagels under the watchful, beady eye of the diminutive Juan, Pablo would breeze in from his three mile run, breathless after the final charge up the hill from the church, his skin glistening. And always I’d remember Marvell’s line about the youthful hue adorning some babe’s flesh like morning dew. After breakfast I’d head out for the library, eager to further my work on plant talk, leaving Pablo to spend the day cocooned in the apartment awaiting his final nymphosis. Often, as I'd wave goodbye at the door, he'd be in close, and I must say rather secretive, consultation with his parrot. These discussions would be in Spanish, a language I didn't speak, and I was never invited to participate.

So I would leave the apartment happily, whistling as I ambled down the hill toward Loring Park, which was lovely in the morning despite the two or three disreputable sleepers curled on benches and the occasional implements of dissipation tossed into flower beds or under trees. Needless to say, I'm attractive and must be wary in such places. Moreover, as I traversed the more shaded section of the park I heard the Dionysian call of those flowers of evil of which Baudelaire wrote. But once I emerged from the park, the clarity of daylight returned.

It was a long walk to the library, and a pleasant one. All along Nicollet Avenue, behind glistening windows, people bought and sold, doctors examined eyes, lawyers prepared their briefs and chefs their entrees. I loved the monolithic grandeur, the metal and glass enormity, of the IDS Building. Its seventy or more stories always inspired in me elaborate fantasies concerning the myriad secret negotiations that its offices concealed. Further down the avenue, where the old Donaldson's department store had outlived its time, an entire block was in a state of intriguing demolition in preparation for some shining advance in the commercial life of the city. And a few blocks to the east, adding to the evidence of the city's prosperity, the Metro Dome bubbled up like a giant soufflé. Perhaps I'd ask Pablo to write an Ode to Commerce.

It was good to be a part of it, if only a small part—good to know that the histories that I compiled on the small businesses of Minnesota (and on the private lives of their owners) would assist prospective buyers in their negotiations. And when my dossiers were not purchased by prospective buyers, it was usually because the management of the business in question had paid me nicely to hit the delete key.

Blessedly, the benighted concept of blackmail, like the ancient belief in witchcraft, had been routed by the recent decisions of our Supreme Court concerning free speech in the world of commerce. Moreover, there is a Gnostic text in which God lightens up and confesses that in some of those other books, especially in those “commandments” (I call them the Ten Suggestions), He was just messing with us. In any case, the dossiers were my work, but also a pleasure, and conversely my research on plant languages was a pleasure that required work. We live in an age of deconstructed categories.

On the morning in question, I stopped by Dick Keller’s office. Dick is a detective who does . . . well, things for me. The lawsuit that I was facing would require that some dirt be tossed in the plaintiff’s direction, and I’d have Keller do the spade work. Moreover, when the dirt accidently landed in a courtroom, Keller was adroit at calling a spade an implement of cultivation. His office was a modest room at the rear of a discount clothing store. As I made my way past tables heaped with jeans and sweatshirts, I wondered what the parrot had been whispering so intensely into Pablo’s ear.

Perhaps a tornado—or two blue tornados with badges in their pockets—had spent the night in Keller’s office. Books had been ripped from shelves, and file drawers had been wrenched from their slots. The computer was gone. Was it my business endeavors that were under investigation? My scientific research? I scuttled back through frayed fashions for the homeless, making time lest the agents of Keller’s disappearance should return.

But Dick’s was only the first of the day’s unforecast departures. Pablo had written in his former life about the necessary impurity of poetry, and when I arrived home in the late afternoon, I learned once again that life is more impure than any poem. The night before, precisely when I was upside down and half way to heaven, the parrot had swooped into the bedroom to whisper in Pablo’s ear. Now Pablo and his parrot were gone, as was the large plasma TV, which we had mounted to the wall in our best imitation of The

Three Stooges, Juan flapping about and chirruping instructions from his perch on a bookshelf.

Their departure had been hasty, as each had left a half-eaten pastry on the kitchen table. We had planned to participate that day in a march against the behavior that provokes police brutality, and that evening, snuggling on the sofa with bowls of popcorn and glasses of chocolate milk, to watch *Buffy*. In my mind I had projected the future for the three of us as a receding strip mall of evenings stocked full of sit coms and forensic detectives. Insanely—for how could he hold a drill?—I imagined that Pablo's beloved parrot was my ex-dentist, Frank, stealing yet another of my loves.

It is strange how often we think that an event is about us, when in fact we are only bit players in plots that begin and end well beyond the boundaries of comprehension—plots hatched under the sodden bridges of Venice and destined for dénouements in the perfumed penthouses of New York. I hoped that the precipitate exit was merely a matter of Pablo having completed his metamorphosis, and I imagined him instructing a team of lawyers in some oak and mahogany inner sanctum.

With this version of things in place in my mind, I forgave him the theft of the TV, realizing that human progress has often been fueled by theft—Prometheus's theft of fire, Eve's of the apple, and our European ancestors' theft of the land that we now inhabit. Property is central to our way of life, and since it has been argued that all property is rooted in theft, I have never believed that theft is inevitably wrong. And I am amazed by people who believe that owning something makes it theirs.

So I wished Pablo well, and his secretive parrot too. But of course some sadness remained, and half an hour later, just to add penury to pain, my lawyer, Dan Ray, phoned to say that I was now being sued by yet another disgruntled businessman. My tolerant view of Pablo wilted like last week's bouquet—perhaps he had ratted me out after all. But hope was nurtured by my image of Dan as a colossal Agassi wielding racquets in both hands, batting my enemies' pathetic serves down the line for easy points. That bubble popped when Dan announced the size of the check that he expected posthaste.

It was open-mic night at *Sylvia's*, and a bespectacled young lady of girth was reading from her dissertation on Rilke. The men in blue were not in attendance. "She was a grad student," Bullet said, "who offed herself about ten years ago—jumped off the same bridge as John Berryman. Her ghost materializes every now and then when the mic's open. They say she killed herself over that dissertation, and now she's still trying to get it right."

Feeling a need for change, I ordered a martini. A green, dismembered eye, red at the center and staked by a toothpick, stared up at me from the oily beverage like a renegade from Argus. I feared that it was an investigative device and glanced about furtively.

I mentioned Pablo's flight, and Bullet and Len negotiated view points. To Len there was nothing strange in Pablo's assent into America's penthouses of power, although he acknowledged that she may have had evil designs on my welfare. Pablo had always been a true believer, and the fact that he had jumped from Marxism to Capitalism was, as Len saw it, relatively trivial. "Whenever you get these true believers," Len affirmed, "people and relationships take a back seat." Pablo had nearly been a presidential candidate in Chile, stepping aside only out of respect of Allende, and Len claimed that he would not be surprised to find Pablo on our own Republican ticket a decade or so down time's river.

"But," Bullet protested, "everyone believes something or other. Being a true believer isn't the issue. What matters is *what* they believe." I felt a vague unease at Bullet's words, but could not pinpoint the reason.

"I can't simple it up for you any more," Len muttered, returning to his gin fizz and cigarette. "You just don't get it."

"I just don't want it," Bullet replied, pushing some of his blond foliage out of his face. I detected private messages encrypted in this exchange, and I briefly contemplated the extent to which so much of social life is a regress of messages within messages. Then it dawned on me that this insight might well have application to botanical languages.

"I'm trying to appeal to your reason," Len protested, slipping into his other self as he spoke, "bu' ol' Lenny doan fin' dat creature nowhere." Clearly, their relationship was still in disrepair, a fact that served to heighten, like certain narcotics that I have tried, the melancholy of my own situation.

I soon tired of the discussion, and my mind began to stir up images of Crystal and Frank flossing together in a cabana in Merida. Had they, too, acquired a feathered companion? The next thing I knew my spiffy Accord was tracking down Nicollet and I was thinking of old Jean Nicolet (many historians prefer the single el), the French explorer who came to America in the seventeenth century to search for the Northwest Passage, discovering Lake Michigan instead. Perhaps Minneapolis would have a Neruda Boulevard one day, but what exactly would his new accomplishment be? And more importantly, how would I be implicated?

As I skirted the south side of Loring Park, I brought the car to a stop across the street from the church. It was a warm summer evening, and one could sit on a bench near the sidewalk and a streetlight, in full view of passing cars, without venturing down the darkening paths into the sordid interior of the park, where a man such as I would certainly attract unwanted attention. Occasionally, as I sat there that night, voices meandered up from the vibrating depths, low and secretive, and I imagined that they were the voices of my own darker instincts.

We are all, I suppose, strangers to ourselves, beings filled with unknown languages and dark alleys. Maybe I should be outraged that Pablo Neruda came back as a bimbo, beaming himself straight into my life and then into . . . what? Corporate power? The FBI? Oblivion? I was a high-school peacenik in the Sixties, bearded (during summer vacation), beaded, and blue-jeaned, someone who went all soft and reverent at the name of Che Guevara, whom Pablo had also known. This history may account for the recent presence of the culture police on the outskirts of my life. But this pronoun "I" that looks so stable and monolithic on the page, as Apollonian as a towering high-rise, is really a site of contradictions and confusions, of constant demolitions and reconstructions—a building like our own IDS tower in which the work force is constantly changing. I am now as proudly conservative as any ranting journalist on Fox TV. Like my musical friend, Len, I'm not ashamed of change. You might as well lament cell division.

I tried to imagine the denizens of Loring Park, their dark needs and desperate transactions conducted in an ancient language almost as foreign as that of flowers. As I leaned back on the bench and tipped my head toward the sky, I perceived their murmurings sifting through the trees just on the threshold of hearing, recalling sounds that I had heard more frequently in the secret gardens of my youth. Perhaps, having noted me under the glow of the streetlight, the night prowlers were desperate for my company.

But to me they were the primitive voices of a past humanity, remnants, perhaps, of God's first draft of what mankind might be—a suffering, yearning brood soon to be replaced in an altogether sunnier future of surveillance and inoculation, of genetic engineering and universal prosperity, a new and brave future where the laments of the old poets would no longer resonate. And, I thought, are not the voices of the past, which is to say the accumulation of cultural traditions warehoused in all the texts that are catalogued in libraries and "taught" in colleges—are these not great inhibitors to spontaneity and joy, and even to progress? Are not businessmen such as I, businessmen who have liberated themselves from the sentimental rules and morals of the past, are we not tomorrow's architects?

The form that approached me from the gloom of the park had fiery hair and one lavender eye from which mist arose as from a pond at dawn. His skirt too was lavender, and he placed one foot carefully in front of the other as he walked, setting his delicious hips into undulant motion. As he took my hand, he hummed an old Cole Porter tune.

"You're gorgeous," he whispered.

"Right back at chya," I suavely chirruped.

He interrupted his musical rendition to suggest that we go for Chinese takeout. Preparing for bed later that night, we stood in front of my bathroom mirror admiring my face, a face marked with cryptic symbols: the graying hair, attesting to wisdom; the lines etched in tanned skin according to the familiar epidermal syntax, speaking of past adventures; and the sharp, blue eyes, minions of an intelligent mind. It was not a face to warrant desertion. I had simply found myself in agendas that not even one such as I could control. Indeed, I felt that my life had become something insubstantial, like a cloud drifting from place to place—from domesticity with Crystal to promiscuity with Pablo. And now? My one-eyed temptress had remained silent since reading his fortune cookie, but the vapor from his solitary lavender eye had a pleasingly intoxicating effect. Who needed words?

On the pillow of the bed that Pablo and I had briefly shared, Puddle Eye and I found a small green feather. It too was a message, but I refused to employ my skills of decipherment, preferring merely to watch it wobble gently through the air and into the wastebasket. I suckled contentedly on the creature from the park, and as a result my sleep was a swirl of blissful images receding down forest paths or down the snowy sides of mountains. The following morning was bright and clear. Not to put too fine a point on it, I felt like many millions of bucks.

The creature had apparently left early—perhaps for a solitary jog, perhaps for a consultation with the culture cops in blue, or maybe even for a journey with Keller, the missing detective, to another world. In my euphoria, I didn't care. I had at last come to terms with my primitive instincts—my attraction not only to *Sylvia's* but to the dark voices murmuring the nights away in Loring Park. Clearly, these instincts could be channeled in the service of commerce and country, and this was the lesson that Pablo and his hook-beaked buddy had been sent to deliver.

Moreover, the respective scatterings of Crystal, Keller, and Pablo and Juan no longer concerned me. I realized that our newly ordered society demands a sanguine attitude toward the disappearance of others—and toward unanswered questions in general. Scientists are not so foolish as to believe that nature will ever yield all of her secrets, and I can see no reason why government should not replicate nature in this regard. One must embrace the mysteries. So as I began my toilette, I realized that it was enough that my work on botanical languages—which our government apparently viewed with a benign eye—awaited me like an old friend at the library, and of course there were dossiers to prepare and plaintiffs to vanquish.

Lathering in the shower, I contemplated my role in the drama of commerce and human progress. Eventually, as I dried myself with my favorite towel, my hooting and laughing subsided. On many occasions I have generously attempted to jam with my neighbor, but on that morning his amateurish, arrhythmic thumping could not be papered over even by my considerable vocal skills. I made my way to the kitchen where I poured orange juice and cracked eggs, a breakfast that I had recently denied myself in consideration of the parrot. I have always been careful to observe such niceties.

Ghosts in the Rain

"Quack! Quack!" Debra ordered as she rummaged on a shelf near the back of the cabin. "Quack?" she asked, holding a small box up for interrogation.

"What, pray tell . . . ?"

"I'm looking for the duck tape. Quack. Quack? Quack, goddamit!" A paperback fell from the shelf, its leaves fluttering like a shot bird.

The cabin, which commanded a half acre lot that sloped down to Island Lake, belonged to Lawrence, my annoyingly upward mobile brother—annoying, that is, until the party for Grandma Lil's eighty-fifth birthday. It was April, which can be a dreary, inadequate month in Minnesota. Rather than taking her outside to see a few trees and clouds, we wheeled Grandma down a graded hall to the lounge of the nursing home to admire the birdcage with its more pleasant version of springtime. As she pushed her time-warped fingers around in cake and ice cream, Lawrence—no Larry for him—announced his plan to amble the summer away in Provence and Tuscany with his new wife, Barbara Stevenson of Stevenson Enterprises, whom he had met in a boss-and-secretary bar near the IDS Building in Minneapolis. While they popped corks in Isle-sur-la-Sorgue or hiked trails in the Luberon, would I care to use the lake cabin?

"You bet your bippy," I said, doing my upbeat thing.

"Mommy, what's a bippy?"

That bit of research was conducted by my niece, the daughter of my older sister, Stacy. Lawrence was twenty-eight then, also my elder. I'm the kid. And at that time I was the black sheep, lagging behind my entrepreneurial siblings, saying *bah* to financial security, and dreaming of spinning a novel from my wooly imaginings. I refused to credit Lawrence's assurances that there is dignity in a day's work, and I dreaded ordinary employment. The common instruction manual for navigating life's rapids offered too many ways to drown, whereas life, I thought, should be a series of magical moments, stepping stones across a creek. A summer with Debra in Lawrence's lakeside cabin would be magical.

Two months later there we were, Debra and I, paddling about in Lawrence's canoe, barbecuing in Lawrence's pit, building fires in Lawrence's fireplace on chill nights, and sporting us like amorous ducks of prey in Lawrence's bed.

"Quackity, quack-quack! I found it!" Debra pivoted and marched off with the tape, a Florence Nightingale about to give first aid—and last aid, as it turned out—to Huey, her rubber ducky. As she disappeared into the bedroom, I admired yet again the tattoo creeping up to peer mischievously over the back of her jeans.

Debra and I had been together three years. I was an MFA candidate in the Dryer College Creative Writing Program. It was that final, hanging around stage—I just needed to finish a collection of stories that would be the triumphant conclusion to my academic grind. I'd be a rubber-stamped writer, and the seas would part. Those who ran the program were a contentious (and horny) assortment of academics and authors, forever rubbing against one another in pain or pleasure. But after only minimal squabbling, they agreed to let me earn chump change teaching a room full of metallically ornamented undergraduates about your plots and your characters, your conflicts and your closure. Not to mention your commas and your semicolons.

Debra sat in the front row. Sometimes, as her contemplation deepened, her finger traced the scar that began in the middle of her cheek and disappeared in a swirl of brown hair. During the third week she materialized, clutching a bouquet of her poems and watercolors, in the doorway of the office that I shared with four other bottom feeders.

So I wasn't a *real* faculty member, something I say to counterpunch my guilt, which has a dynamite left hook. I was raised a Lutheran in a small Minnesota town, where guilt came at you right from the start. In my corner of the heartland, public displays of affection were reserved for rare occasions, as when a certified next of kin is saved from the teeth of an especially large Bengal tiger.

For Debra, on the other hand, the kisses hello and goodbye were as normal as breathing. I'd glance about desperately as we met for lunch in Coffman Union, feeling the great weight of Midwestern judgment settle on my shoulders. At each turn of the conversation, as her fingers played in my hair or rested affectionately on my arm, I'd check my watch or turn the back of my head to a colleague that I'd spotted across the room. The semester was a curious blend guilt and joy.

Debra's family had moved up from Louisiana to market Cajun food products in the Midwest, and her Tabasco-seasoned blood pumped to a different beat than mine. Her hair and eyes were a deep, beckoning brown, her poems small and lovely. I came to suspect that there were no inhibitions down on the bayou, and I would imagine her at a *fais dodo* by Barataria Bay, the sun setting and her hair flying as she dances barefoot in the dust. I'd see her raising moonshine to her lips in an old fruit jar, the arm of someone named Bruneau or Thibodeaux looped about her waist as a fiddle lilts in the distance.

Once the sun was down in our more decorous northern city and we were safely ensconced in my apartment in Dinky Town, as they call the neighborhood by the college, Debra was Keats's tender night, and I did my best to stumble through her "verdurous glooms and winding mossy ways."

Thankfully, the teaching only lasted one semester. By the summer on Island Lake, Debra and I had been together three years. My novel swelled in the circuitry of my laptop between eight and eleven each morning and—when hiking, boating, or entertaining friends up from the Twin Cities didn't intrude—between two and four in the afternoon. It concerned the music scene in Minneapolis, and I had invented characters who had chilled with Prince or whose parents had hitched across the country blowing pot with Bob Dylan. Debra too had an intriguing museum of fictional friends, and I started to envy the easy way that she lived in an imagined world.

Sometimes she'd come in from a midnight walk, place the battery-operated lantern on the nightstand, and claim that she had been searching for an imaginative man. Then, to soften it, she'd smile and say, "I mean an even more imaginative man." One night she informed me that she was "the Diogenes of the Visionary." Then she did her sexpot pout and flipped off the lantern. Falling to sleep, she gave my hair a quick stroke and whispered, "Little lamb, who made thee?"

Actually, I knew that she often wandered off for late-night visits to a retired dancer, who lived by herself a quarter of a mile down the shore. But for weeks the imagination issue squirmed around in our bedding and lingered on the sun deck during morning coffee. What can I say? Each chapter of my novel arrived stillborn, and it became apparent that when it came to imagination, I drove a compact.

As if to counterpoint my literary efforts—perhaps dipping her paddle into the still water on a cool summer morning, or gazing from the deck out across the lake and into the dreamscape of a cloudy afternoon—she'd offer scenes from her life as a ghost.

"I remember sitting with Bill," she told me one rainy evening, referring to the pianist Bill Evans, who died in 1980, around the time that Debra was born. But it was 1946 in Debra's story. "I remember sitting with Bill on the screened porch of my uncle's camp on a bayou near Hammond. We watched the rain hurry toward us down the bayou to rustle in the cypress and the oaks and then come as mist through the torn screen. Then Bill said that whenever it rains you can remember every time that it's ever rained."

As Debra spoke, I recalled a rain-blurred Saturday from my childhood when I had waited for my father under a theater marquee after my parents' divorce. He had forgotten to pick me up.

"What sneaks inside you in the rain," she continued, "isn't something alien—it's what you've always been but may have forgotten. Rain settles into the grooves of your mind and pulls music out, like a needle in an old stereo. I was twenty in 1946, a sophomore, and Bill was 17. He had already had a few gigs in New Jersey, but was in Louisiana to study music theory at Southeastern—of all places! He thought he'd become a teacher, but I could see him heading for performance. And sure as poop, he became the brooding white guy in the world of heroin and smoke. We dated for a few months. When he left Hammond I went to the bottom of the bayou. It's really slimy down there. Yuk."

Words like "poop" and "yuk" signaled the end of her ghostly imaginings and a return to her everyday self. Then, perhaps, she'd comb my hair with her fingers.

"Teddy, Teddy burning bright," she might croon, "what are we going to do with you? Your hair looks like a cypress swamp after a hurricane. And those beady, alligator eyes! Have you ever seen an alligator's eyes floating on the surface of a bayou? Were you formed to remind me of home?"

But then she might turn from me quickly, almost with revulsion, and return to her life as a ghost. I remember her talking of Ellaine.

"Ellaine was okay, with her cats and dogs and hippy slacks, although a junky needs another junky like that bug on your shoe needs a can of Raid. I'd float in the doorway sometimes as they lay tangled in one another after heroin or sex. Once Bill's eyelids fluttered and I knew that he'd seen me. He whispered, 'Who's there?' When Bill left Ellaine to marry Nenette, Ellaine killed herself too, belly flopping in front of a New York subway."

One rainy night, in front of the fire in the cabin, Debra described haunting the recording sessions Bill did with Miles Davis, the sessions that produced *Kind of Blue*.

"They recorded in an abandoned church in New York that had become the 30th Street Studio for Columbia Records. Hovering in the corner, I was a shadow within a shadow. As he played, I could see Bill's thoughts swirl about him in the air like smoke." And then, suddenly back in the present with the rain droning on the cabin roof, she said, "I've spent so much of my life in the rain. Always the same rain."

On another evening—we were paddling in the canoe under moonlight—she imagined herself in Webster Hall in 1968 when Bill recorded *Alone* for Verve.

"Scott LaFaro, his first bassist, had died in a car wreck. Bill's left arm was half paralyzed from hitting a nerve with a needle. It was so stupid, that whole heroin thing. He was underweight and sullen, with hepatitis and malnutrition. I cried my little, invisible ghost tears, and as he shuffled up to the piano I whispered to him about the bayou and the rain. He sat down and played 'Here's That Rainy Day,' the notes weaving patterns into the silence like mist on a lake, or stars in the void. A few years later Bill wrote a piece called 'Turn Out the Stars'."

Our canoe drifted, paddles stowed, as Debbie fell silent. I thought about all the myriads of stars and wondered why the night sky isn't a solid sheet of light. I don't know why there is darkness.

There was the time, back when I taught commas and colons, when I had asked her about the scar that twisted upward into her hair. What was *it* a ghost of? Her face darkened, and I never asked again. On the other hand, she talked a lot about the darkest moments of her ghostly life. Debra's stories about Bill Evans were a forest of details in which her real self became as lost as any child in a fairy tale.

It is hard to imagine Debra's attraction to Evans himself, to the addicted, undernourished and sullen human animal. When I asked her about it once, about the distance between the beautiful music and the flawed person, she gazed at me with disappointed incredulity. Evans had managed to translate depression, disease and pain into beauty, and that alchemy was all that mattered to Debra. But her imagined hauntings of Bill Evans seemed perverse to me, a strange parody of intimacy, almost an imagined stalking. His life had been a slow unfolding of sadness through the years—always the same rain. In her imagination, she had made herself a part of it.

She talked about his friend, Philly Joe Jones, the drummer, and how Jones got Bill back on heroin after a two or three year recovery. She mentioned Eddie Gomez, the bassist, who was there when Evans died. "At the end, Bill coughed blood and struggled to perform, dying in a taxi cab as they rushed him to a hospital in a frenzy of hepatitis, ulcers, and pneumonia."

A couple of evenings before Debbie left me we had navigated the county road to *Captain Kidd's*, a brass-and-rope fish house on the far side of the lake. I had spilled my wine while checking my new watch—a Mickey Mouse that Debra had given me—and finished my broiled walleye brooding about my inability to transmute my clumsiness into art in the manner of Debbie's fabled lover. I was sure that deep and wonderful things were being said at the other tables in the room, while all that I could talk about was global warming or the declining fish population in the lakes. Later, as we walked to our car, the big dipper poured its mysterious brew into our atmosphere.

Back at the cabin we sprawled in front of the fire. On the wall above it, a head with soaring antlers stared its permanent stare. Eventually Debra, rearranging herself among pillows, told me that after Bill's death she'd decided to haunt the world in the rain. She had already floated down rain-drenched trails in the Green Mountains of Vermont and had stretched herself thin on the deck of a small boat under a summer shower in Brittany.

"There's a beauty to rain in forgotten places," she mused, "in bays where ships no longer go, in ghost towns, in abandoned drive-in theaters, with maybe just a section of the screen standing and a few corroded posts still lying in the grass that wraps itself around them.

"One rainy day in Portland I drifted into a small restaurant, passing through an old woman hesitating in the doorway, gray and dripping, nearly a ghost herself. Inside, they were playing a tape of one of Bill's concerts in Paris. The old woman wilted onto a stool at the counter, and I stared at her from an empty chair, watching the memories swirl around her head like clouds. Time had abandoned her. I wondered if, had I lived, I would have attained a lovely loneliness like hers. Then I drifted away, passing a young couple huddled under an umbrella on the sidewalk, in love for a while."

The logs of the fire had crumbled into intricate, glowing passageways. Here and there in the flames, a vermilion eye emerged and vanished or a ghoulish tongue dangled from a snarling lip. When I poked the embers, sparks swarmed away like wasps from a nest.

"You live more in the imagination than I can," I said, tossing on another log.

"Yes, my sensible Teddy, my little lamb burning bright, you've got too much respect for the real."

It was true. There were times when I thought that her mind might go on one of its hauntings and not return, so little did the everyday negotiations of life matter to her. But lying with her by a fire in a darkened room was magical. I remember thinking that such moments and the feelings they bring can't be clung to or planned, that trying to represent them in words is as futile as chasing a scent with a butterfly net. They move in their own dimension, touching us now and then with the soft wings of yearning and ecstasy. I'd been wrong to think I could live an enchanted life by force of will.

Debra's ghostly self sometimes mingled with the quackity-quack self that I observed on the morning of her vanishing. Deb had poles of beauty and silliness, like the lantern and the duck. I continued tapping my own fantasies into the laptop until well after noon on the day of the duck-tape search, but as hunger set in I began to miss Debbie. I don't mean in any serious way—it was just a matter of whether I should crack out the ham and the mustard now or wait for company. Hunger prevailed, but as the afternoon poked along, a fissure formed in the day that no tape could close. When I checked my watch for the third or fourth time and found that Mickey's gloved hands had slipped past three o'clock, I decided to look around.

I walked down the shore to Katrina's house, my feet making shallow impressions in the sand-and-pebble beach. Katrina, the elderly *danseuse*, had once worked with the likes of Balanchine and Graham. I had first seen her one afternoon standing on her dock for many minutes, still as a piece by Rodin. It's strange how interesting strangers can be when seen from a distance, without the encumbrance of real circumstances—a job, relationships, opinions, anxieties. My imagination invents exotic lives for them, but I'm usually disappointed if I come to know someone whom my fantasies have decorated and flocked like a Christmas tree.

Katrina was not on her dock that day, so I climbed the steps from the shore, passed through the screened porch, and knocked. Debra? That dark-eyed girl who had known Bill Evans? No, she didn't think that she had seen her today, although they had had a wonderful conversation recently. Maybe it was last night. I accepted Katrina's invitation to come in.

"I told her all about my marvelous years in Paris," Katrina said as we settled into a floral-designed sofa that threatened to devour us like a great, carnivorous plant. "Do you know, I had this thing with Gato Barbieri, the jazzman? But of course you wouldn't know. He was—how do you say—a handful of *merde*, many times. There is a jazz *cave* on *rue Descartes*, where we fell in love. It was mad, the folly of my life."

Her eyes had shifted into that time-traveling gear, and I wondered at how much of life is spent reinventing one's past.

"I knew James Baldwin there. Do you remember his books? And Anaïs Nin—did you ever meet Anaïs? She was a little . . . goofy. I like that word. He was a silly dog in a comic book, Goofy, *n'est-ce pas*? Oh, and there were so many others in Paris. You must go to Paris and meet everyone."

Her hand indicated the walls, which were a collage of photographs in dusty frames—pictures from inside dance studios and restaurants, formal pictures artfully posed or candid ones snapped on the street in front of a *Tabac* or along the Seine. Recognizing Pablo Picasso among a boisterous crowd in a restaurant, I remembered how my mother had sold the signed lithographs that had hung in our front hall after reading about Picasso's shoddy treatment of women. Once, during a Florida vacation years ago, I had ordered flounder.

"Is that the fish with both eyes on one side?" my mother had asked.

"I don't know," I confessed.

"Well, I don't want you eating anything designed by Picasso," she had warned, smiling over her Manhattan.

Katrina brought me back to the present with her claim that the person holding her hand in the Luxembourg Garden was Marguerite Duras, the novelist. I examined the living Katrina more closely, noting the cheek bones and the willowy poise that must have passed for coin of the realm in some gone decade on the *rive gauche*. I tried to explain that I was worried about Debra—that I hadn't seen her since morning.

"*Alors*, isn't your Debra the one that's the ghost? Yes. She's the ghost who came here sometimes at night with the lantern. We'd talk and talk. Such a sweet ghost, *tres joli*. You can't find her? Maybe you should look in the rain."

"Yes, but . . . ." She ignored my attempt at a response.

"Do you remember that poem by Paul Verlaine? I will translate its beginning—'it cries in my heart like it rains on the town.' Only *cries* and *rains* and *heart* are all connected by sound in French. And in the next lines the sound of *languor* seems to embrace *coeur*. So that these things wash together in the poem—tears and rain and languor and heart.

Il pleure dans mon coeur
Comme il pluet sur la ville;
Quelle est cette langueur
Qui penetre mon coeur?

Do you see? In any case, you should look for your Debra where it rains. The heart lives most intensely in the rain."

As she talked about the heart, her small hands gripped the cushions of the sofa as if the spinning earth meant to fling her away. But I was getting nowhere. Glancing around the room, I noticed a cello propped in the corner.

"I used to play the cello, you know," Katrina said. "Sometimes you needed to relax your feet from the dance, and those were the times for the cello. I didn't do that on stage, though. Cello was just for me, *seulement*. I don't do it any more. Now I need to relax everything." She raised hands that were twisted and knotted like roots. "I need to relax even my heart. My problems have never been problems of money," she said, "but problems of the heart."

The lake lapped and whispered on the shore as I returned to the cabin. A heron posed on one leg in the water, and beyond it, in a row boat, an elderly couple cast fishing lines at the edge of a floating island of lily pads. Further off, six or seven people lounged with drinks on a pontoon boat, their voices soft and clear on the water. Entering the back door of the cabin, I paused by the shelf where Debbie had rummaged for the duck tape, and recalled that she had taken it, quacking madly, into the bedroom. There, I found some photos of us with a few friends who had visited the lake recently. They were duck-taped to the walls, maybe in imitation of Katrina's hangings. Also taped to the wall was her goodbye.

> *Some ghosts come back to earth for love or revenge, or because there's something to purge. I came back for the rain and the music, and for the lost places where you feel time's undertow. It isn't your fault that I can't feel it now—it's just how it is with ghosts. We dull easy—hey, we're just knives carved from soap. Like poetry, love requires imagination, and mine is fading. It's time for me to turn out the stars. Take care of my rubber ducky, who has a bobo on his tummy. Good luck with that novel!*

I pondered the exuberant exclamation point. Clearly, both Debbies, the sublime one and the silly one, inhabited the letter. Below the goodbye, on the nightstand by the lantern, Huey recuperated with a large, silver bandage around his midsection.

I have an ordinary heart, which broke in the ordinary way—some self-destructive cigarette smoking, which I've since abandoned, solitary walks by the lake, and a number of nights bumping into tables and chairs at The Crow Bar, clutching a bottle like a kid with a joystick, finally to be shooed off into the darkness along with the remnants of the 4x4 and motorcycle crowd, the sort of crowd that materializes uncannily at saloons that operate miles from anywhere. There were tears in my heart, like the mist on the lake.

In a few days I cleared out. As I said, I was raised in a culture of guilt. So I worried about Katrina. She had told us that she spends the winter at the lake, and I wondered how she managed. I knew that she had groceries delivered, and I had noticed the same blue Buick in her driveway from time to time during the summer, so someone apparently looked in on her. With these reminders, I was able to absolve myself of responsibility.

When we said goodbye, Katrina nodded and asked if I wanted orange juice. We sat for a few minutes among her pictures, and I asked if Debra had mentioned where she might go after her stay at the lake. Oh yes, Debra had mentioned so many places. It was difficult to remember them all. As Katrina spoke, she gazed at the walls. I was sure that Debra's places, if they had been mentioned at all, had mingled in Katrina's mind with her own lost world, yesterday's Paris, sustained by longing after so many years. Patiently, I awaited the muffled thud of dropping names, but Katrina remained silent. A few minutes later I left.

The highway to Minneapolis was a shimmering mirage in the August heat, the side-roads, vacant of cars, clicking by like great, fallen poles. I slowed into various vague towns with signs assuring the traveler that he was entering A MINNESOTA STAR CITY. By what obscure process are such honors conferred? Do dignitaries come to town? Is there a parade? Speeches in the park? Fireworks? So much of America remains a mystery to me.

I moped around in Minneapolis for a month, satisfying myself that none of our friends was covering Debra's footprints. During that time Lawrence dangled a job at Lakeside Industries in front of my nose, and, like a dutiful bass, I nibbled. Lakeside was a new operation that Stevenson Enterprises was launching up in Duluth. Barbara, my sister-in-law, was the gatekeeper. The interview with Barbara's uncle occurred over lunch at the Athletic Club. He was well-upholstered in an expensive suit and silk tie, but his talk was informal and friendly. I was hired. On my way up to Duluth, I stopped at Island Lake to check on Katrina.

It was early October. The trees at Island Lake were gaudy, and the water's gooseflesh came and went under the breeze. An elderly couple leaned together in the doorway of Katrina's house like friendly old cattle.

"Well no," the woman said when I asked about Katrina. "Carl and I purchased this house in September."

"We got it for a song," Carl added, "only a few days after it went on the market."

He smiled contentedly under sparse strands of hair lotioned to his scalp like seaweed on a rock. The walls behind them were freshly painted and hung with a few lithographs and etchings. The man-eating sofa had been wrestled out and hauled away, perhaps to be examined by science. The new owners knew nothing about Katrina's whereabouts. Having worked through an agent, they had never laid eyes on her.

"But you could check with the ReMax people in Duluth," the lady added. "I'm sure they could help you."

Katrina had lived in the past, submerged there like a rare, deep-sea flower. But now, in the present, something had happened. I thanked the new residents, wondering what secret romance or tragedy *they* might star in, then I followed the brick walk to my car, parked by a dying birch.

I was a lost puppy that first, gray November in Duluth, sulking around in the year's spilled ashes. But it passed. I have an office now above the Lakewalk in Duluth, with a large window looking out over an ever changing assortment of joggers, dog walkers and cyclists in skin-tight Spandex. Beyond is Lake Superior, and about ten miles across (this is merely the narrow tip of the lake) the trees of the Wisconsin shoreline blur off over the horizon to the east. Except for a few brutal days in winter it's pleasant here, and I enjoy my work. We make educational products for children—toys, games, and plastic computers. I'm the public relations department, overseeing an advertising budget and making presentations to retail outlets and schools around the Upper

Midwest. I spoke with members of the Education Department at the University of Wisconsin in Madison last week. We make an honest living here at Lakeside, and my guilt detector has remained silent. I became a Diogenes of the Normal, and my search has paid off. There's purpose in the work I do, and I'm grateful to Barbara and Larry—I call him Larry now.

My friends in Duluth include a pharmacist named Hal and his companion, Amanda. Amanda is a publishing author, a fact that I found awkward at first in view of my own abandoned aspirations. The novel that absorbed me that summer at Island Lake went nowhere and languishes on aging paper and in decaying disks; only three stories from my MFA thesis ever crossed the publication threshold, finding their way like refugees into the most remote outposts of literary culture.

But I began to fit in fine with Hal and Amanda the evening—it was after seeing the film about Sylvia Plath at the multiplex—when they renewed their periodic debate as to whether the pill is mightier than the pen. They enjoyed messing with each other about it, and Hal claimed to be writing an essay to be called "Is the Poetic Sensibility Treatable?" I marshaled my forces and offered that the toy just might trump both pill and pen, since nothing is so formative of the young mind and therefore of the future of civilization. My argument was elaborate, with just the right amount of silliness. So now, despite my history of wine spilling, I'm a regular guest at their home. They are friends I can depend on.

It's been a mystery how Debra orchestrated her departure that day. She must have smuggled her duffel bag right under my nose as I tapped away at my doomed novel, or tossed it out the bedroom window like a damsel fleeing the wicked prince. I imagine that a ride waited for her on the county road, and that thought raises images of her on the cell phone out among the trees during the days before her flight—unless she used Katrina's phone. Or maybe she was truly a ghost and just went *poof*.

Debra's lantern, its batteries long dead, stands sentinel on the end of a book shelf in my office, next to some stuff that I've been reading on child psychology, and the rubber duck squats on my window sill. I'm pleased to report that Huey's silver bandage still holds, although I don't really recall the extent of his original "bobo," as the Cajuns say. I'm also pleased to say that I've nearly rid myself of the feeling that Debra is watching as I return to my darkened apartment after a movie or a visit. But, because some things never end, I sometimes feel a breath on my neck as I lie tangled in my sheets in the moments before sleep. And once, drifting to sleep, I saw a presence in the doorway and I whispered, "Who's there?" Presences from the other world still brush me with their wings, but I don't dwell on it.

Perhaps I'll find Debra's poems in print one day, and I imagine a volume with one of her watercolors gracing the cover. I've looked for it in bookstores, almost convinced it exists. And when I look for Debra in my mind—whether the human Debra with the unmentionable scar, or the ghostly Debra who loved Bill Evans—she mingles with my own lost aspirations until she becomes the signifier of art itself, that alternate dimension where it always rains and where apparitions—I almost said aspirations again—where apparitions live their lives of churning intensity.

I don't know why a ghost like Debra bothered haunting me. I don't know what she saw in my plain-as-bread life. Was I one of those lost things that intrigued her? I'm puzzled, and I wonder if Debbie has learned to live more at ease in reality, although I don't know exactly what that means. Even the simplest life is made of fantasies, memories, hopes, and dreams—and then there's the surreal world of elderly people like Katrina. So perhaps the real world is as difficult to grasp as any imagined one.

I think of Debbie's scar, and then I think that she damaged herself by fixing so relentlessly on the unattainable. Or was her fictional life with the dead musician itself a bandage for some other damage to her soul or self? As for myself, I no longer romanticize the unknown. Strangers speaking in hushed tones at remote tables in restaurants are not saying mysterious things—not unless baseball scores and stock prices are windows on Nirvana. I don't read much fiction, and I doubt if music will be as beautiful again as it once was.

I'm not a scientist who can explain why there is darkness in spite of all the stars, and I'm not a poet whose tragic sensibilities blow and swirl across the page. Grandma Lil is gone, Lawrence is worth millions, and I'm thirty-one now. I sell things made of plastic, and I do it for money. It isn't romantic nor adventuresome. When books and movies depict the heightened realities inhabited by poets and painters, these characters are like ghosts in the rain—they don't live in my world. In my world, now, Robert Frost was selfish and mean, and Katrina's Paul Verlaine was pathetic, leaving his family so he could wallow in the mud with Rimbaud. To me, salvation lies in ordinary, dependable things.

When I swivel toward my window, prop my feet up by Huey, and listen to, say, Bill Evans play "My Foolish Heart," my longings are vague. The yearning that flows in my veins is just enough to feel, like that second beer as you watch TV in the evening. Just enough to feel, but not enough to change anything. I'll never be a character in a great adventure. Mine is the world of ducks, not lanterns. Sometimes, picturing Debra and me there by the lake, I wonder if she had been sent to cure me. Maybe she had left the bandaged duck—little Huey, the gallant survivor—as an emblem of the ordinary life that I had to accept. I wonder, and then I check with the mouse on my wrist and get back to work.

A Tale of Autumn and Spring

Sometimes I think of Hal and Amanda as bookends embracing a motley assortment of tales about life in my newly adopted city, tales, unfortunately, that do not always take truth as their first obligation. The fact that they told me about Billy on the evening that Amanda read aloud from her new book of fictions adds to the doubts that I have about Billy's tale. Moreover, although my version of the story is generally what I was told, I've had to imagine many of the particulars. I think of this story not as a history, but more as one of those plastic toys for children that I spend my working hours marketing. While it may have some use, *caveat emptor*.

For instance, I imagine my friends in their breakfast nook that overlooks a hillside cluttered with houses that jostle their way down to Lake Superior. Perhaps it is this altitude that prompts Amanda, Hal's friend of three years, to remind him that a hundred people hurtled themselves from the windows and ledges of the World Trade Center. Hal doesn't respond, musing, as he cuts a bagel, that anthrax can't be far behind. Other morbid topics, such as mad cow disease, industrial pollution, and the destruction of the aquifer, have also festered recently in Amanda's conversation. Maybe, Hal thinks, it's Paxil time.

Needing no encouragement, our heroine plunges into the mysteries of architecture and engineering that produced the modern high-rise. Hal nods absently and reaches for the orange juice, conjuring a mental video of the angular redhead with the tattooed ankle and stiletto heels who ornaments the Cosmetics counter at Target. Hal works in Pharmacy, located adjacent to Cosmetics as if to offer alternate services to the flesh.

"Did you notice any sucking?" Hal asks, gesturing with his juice glass toward the manuscript on the table uncomfortably close to a smear of grape jelly. His question serves to banish the disturbing ankle and also to deflect the conversation from the ills of the world.

The manuscript is a collection of narrated drawings nestled in a brown envelope, Billy Carlson's fledgling graphic novel, tentatively titled *Morph Man*. Knowing that Amanda writes stories, sends them to publishers, and even occasionally sees them printed, Billy approached Hal, extended the envelope in a trembling hand, and asked if he and Amanda would "check if it sucks." Billy is a homely kid, I vaguely remember seeing him myself at Target, with a small oval body that careens about on bent twigs.

The autobiographical roots of Billy's efforts are apparent, but the branches and leaves cast intricate shadows. "The kid can draw," as Hal says to Amanda. The protagonist of *Morph Man* is Clark, who, on the first page, falls in love with a girl he views at a distance, beyond paddling ducks and children at play, in the neighborhood park. This event incites Clark's pursuit of transformation. With the aid of potions supplied by a nerdy chemistry student, Clark toils each morning before his Colgate-spattered mirror, prodding and tugging himself into new creations. One day he emerges from the bathroom with enormous arms, another day with wings and a forehead that sports a giant horn. He can pull his ears out to the size of a satellite dish, and he learns to assume the shapes of various animals. Each night during sleep, Clark's body returns to normal, or rather to its own original form, becoming raw material for the next morning's efforts.

But Clark fails to become a superhero. Despite its new shapes, his body maintains its old limitations—it still limps, erupts in pimples and boils, and emits gases with alarming frequency. He doesn't dare to show himself in public, spending his days moping in his dingy apartment, perhaps opening a can of soup with his talons or dusting the Gibson guitar with his feathers. The one shape that Clark can't achieve is that of an average American man. Billy's graphic novel divides its time between Clark's fantasy exploits and his actual despair. He'll never win the damsel in the park.

"I thought the ending was touching," Hal says.

"I read it," Amanda replies. "It's good, especially the drawings. Graphic novels have potential—as a form, I mean."

"Guess I'll take it back to him today. I suppose he wants us to say something constructive, Darling. Would you mind being brilliant for a minute or two?"

"Tell him that he jazzes the old comic-book conventions nicely. But I'd lose some of Clark's self-pity. And you're wrong about the end. It should tie in better with Clark's need for love—you can't just kill off your character like that."

"Don't kill him off. Gotchya. Ta-ta, Darling."

As Hal turns his Corolla down the hill toward the lake, he remembers the old question of whether a falling tree in a forest makes sound if no one is there to hear. More curious, I imagine Hal musing, is the question of whether a man making a statement out of the hearing of his female companion is still wrong.

At noon, dodging carts pushed by desperate children and distracted parents through the mazes of the store, Hal navigates the aisles to Electronics to find Billy. They buy burgers and fries and head out to the pond and play area across the highway, where the mothers of the city air their endless supple of toddlers. They find a bench, and Billy grunts as he scratches near the metal pellet implanted in his nose. He sits, his feet barely reaching the ground, and cranks his head upward toward Hal.

"I just want to check. I mean, they got nose jobs and implants and stuff. I bet they're working on the chemistry end too. They already got steroids. Why not pills to change the shape of the body? Why not zap certain parts of the body with certain pills? They already got a pill to get your wang hard, so how about one for a straight nose or a larger chin? You do any research like that, maybe in your spare time? I was askin' the other pharmacist, but he zipped his burger trap. Maybe it's a military secret?"

"I'm not a researcher, Billy. I just sell the stuff. I really don't know what's happening in that area. I'm not saying it's impossible, but I don't think the science is that far along."

Billy's mouth is too occupied with a clump of French fries to protest, and Hal hurries on to praise the satire in *Morph Man*, conscious of the nose ornament staring back at him.

"I mean, you surround Clark with all these supposedly normal people who have pierced thises and tattooed thats and augmented whadyacallits. You're talking about how this whole beauty thing is becoming invasive. When I was a kid dying your hair was a big deal. You're really onto social change here. And then . . . ."

"So the drugs are Top Secret?"

Later, walking in silence back to Target, Hal ponders Billy's search for transformation. Pharmacy and Cosmetics, he knows, are drifting closer like stars caught in each other's gravity. It's a topic that the three of us discussed on the first evening that they had me to their place for dinner, shortly after the romantic disappointment that precipitated my move to Duluth.

I imagine Hal asking, after giving the evening meal a chance to settle out of harm's way, if Amanda has heard of people collecting body parts via the Internet. "I suppose it was just more of Billy's nuttiness, but he was saying that some people lop off fingers and toes and send them to one another."

"It's true," Amanda says, tossing Hal a dish towel and

motioning him to get busy. "There was something about it on *Nova* the other night, along with people who try to operate on their own brains. It's called trapenation or trepanation—something like that. The ground zero of self-improvement."

"So Billy's on the cutting edge of culture."

"Cutting indeed. But Love Machine, you think that my concern with safety issues is morbid, and here you are talking about trading body parts. I'm going to take away your comic books."

Three hours later, as Hal prepares for bed before the bathroom mirror, he scrutinizes the hints of gray infiltrating the hairs above his ears and wonders if vanity will also cause him to succumb to chemical solutions.

A procedural note. If I don't describe the tender labors of the boudoir, the hasty reader shouldn't assume that they're absent from the lives of our protagonists, also my friends. These days, opening the cover of a novel is too often like opening the door of a bedroom to confront an epic contest *in media res*. Instead, I'll adopt the more dignified conventions of an earlier time. We're Hal and Amanda's guests, after all, and courtesy is a higher value than graphic prose. So, before decency is further compromised, let's tiptoe down the hall and bid one another a pleasant *bon soir*, each retiring to his of her own nocturnal beeswax.

Two days pass of rain and brisk wind, of trees hunching their shoulders and keening away. When May unveils the sun again, Hal strolls over to Cosmetics, where the local nymphs, as he calls them, converge to buy their weapons. He pauses in the perfumed air to make a lunch date with Shasta. As they talk, he imagines a scene like one he had contemplated on the embossed cover of a romance novel by the checkout line.

An hour later, a matronly duck and her darlings scurry toward the pond as Shasta chooses a bench in the shade of one of Minnesota's last giant elms.

"Really, he's *so* creepy," Shasta declares. "He's always hanging around Panties trying to get my attention. I can't imagine why." Hal fails to fill the silence in the sought-after way, so Shasta continues. "And did you notice that the last time we had lunch he was sitting across the pond just staring at us, like he's hatching a plot?" As she shoves a straw through the lid of her shake, Hal realizes that he is the chemistry nerd and Shasta is the elusive damsel of Billy's art.

"No," Hal says, "I didn't notice. But don't be too hard on Billy. He's kind of lonely right now. Someone needs to help him out of his shell."

"Hey Kids!" It's Waxman from Hardware, finishing his daily half hour of dork-walking around the pond, oblivious to the children who delight in his flailing arms.

"Meltin' those pounds off, Wax?" Shasta calls.

"Didjya hear the noon news?" Waxman asks, pausing by the bench. "Some kid jumped off the Bong Bridge. Even money it's that goof in Electronics. He hasn't been to work in two days."

"Jesus, Wax," Shasta says, "you don't have to sound so cheerful about it."

"Sorry," Waxman sings, resuming his Pythonesque stroll, "didn't mean to sound cheerful."

"What a ghoul," Shasta declares. She quickly relents, leaning toward Hal and whispering words that smell of cigarettes and Listerine, and elevates "Weird Waxie" to the level of "dickhead." Then she squints at her watch. "What time ya got?" she asks. When Hal replies, she announces in that cryptic modern way that "we gotta run."

For the remainder of the afternoon, Hal gives mixed reviews to his romantic, sun-drenched interlude in the park, deciding, as he applies a usage label to a tube of Zovirax, that cheating on your girl isn't all it's cracked up to be.

Eyeballing Shasta. A curl, coyly straying from its sisters, falls across her tanned forehead, directing attention to the green eyes that, with great frequency, conduct disturbing encounters throughout our sedate city. On her blouse, a button likewise declines its conventional duties, revealing to the vigilant viewer the soft and provocative glandular companions (called "boobs" in the current demotic) that rise and fall beneath the chic-but-affordable fabric, a fabric that poutingly refuses to reach its lower destination, thus displaying that currently eroticized scar, the navel, pierced and spangled *a la mode*. Continuing our descent and hastily completing our inventory (lest gentle readers take offense), we will merely note the delightfully snug and tattered jeans selected from Target's extensive collection.

For the usual reasons of delicacy, the evening news withholds the name of the deceased, but the commentator's mention of wings is all that Hal needs. A woman on the bridge, pausing to admire the harbor during her walk from Minnesota to Wisconsin, reported seeing a young man wrestle some paraphernalia from a duffel bag, strap it to his shoulders, and disappear over the rail. Judging from his choice of a launch site, he wasn't concerned to hit water. It was speculation, but the investigating officer guessed that the "mess" on train tracks below included makeshift wings.

"Like Icarus," Hal observes, perhaps envisioning something by Picasso, flattened and disconnected.

"Yes," Amanda agrees. "It makes you wonder what elusive sun poor Billy thought he could reach."

The next morning a wizened man in Hardware tells the inquiring officer that Billy once mentioned an addicted mother in

Minneapolis. But two days of official rummaging in that city fail to produce either parent. On the third morning after the plunge, Hal passes the hat at Target, then drives to a nearby funeral home. There he meets with a portly funeral director, hermetically sealed in a gray business suit, starched collar, and blue tie, to arrange for a visitation and cremation.

Later, at Billy's apartment, really just a bedroom in a marginal neighborhood, Hal confronts a blizzard of socks and underwear and a wreckage of pill bottles and lotions. Posters of sports cars and bikini babes cling precariously to the walls, and from behind the walls dead rodents emit a pungent revenge. Hal retrieves *Morph Man* and an ancient Gibson guitar. These tokens of Billy's life and aspirations are displayed for the 15 or 20 Target employees who brave a rainy night to give Billy's departure a small portion of dignity.

Shasta, the nymph of perfumes and creams, and Weird Waxie, are there, the two drifting into subdued conversation near the donations box. Hushed surmises as to Billy's motivations flutter like moths about the rented, and closed, plastic casket. Apparently the mortician despaired of putting Billy together again. Hal and Amanda, whispering by themselves in a corner, conclude that an understanding of Billy's quest for an impossible self is best left to trained professionals. The visitation runs its course.

The next day Hal places a check in a chubby hand and receives the ceramic vase containing the reduced and dehydrated particles that had once been Billy.

It's the day of Amanda's book signing, her maiden voyage between hard covers, and it is also the day that I first heard Billy's story. When Hall arrives home, pausing to place the vase on a shelf of an oak cabinet near the front entrance, Amanda is reading aloud to the pictures on the wall. Lake Superior Writers has secured a room at St. Scholastica College, and three people will read from and autograph, no doubt with exaggerated swirls and arabesques, their newly published volumes. Amanda's book is a collection of short stories, but before reading from it she will offer something of her newest and as yet unpublished story, "The Ambivalent Spring." It begins:

> *It was an April of soft showers that lingered in fields or drifted carelessly over hills and down country roads. But Carol, viewing springtime's return from the window of her breakfast room, was a realist. The newspaper on the table told of the death of a child, and two weeks ago, on an evening of crumbling regrets, Carol's father had passed away in the family house in Baton Rouge. The robin returns to the cemetery, she mused, as well as to the farm, and Chaucer's pilgrims went in search of a dead man. Carol wondered, pouring her second cup of coffee, what commerce her own impending journey would have with death or renewal.*

"That's terrific, Darling, a wonderful beginning—lovely, dark, and deep, as the poet said. You'll knock 'em dead."

"You're a sweetheart, Sweetheart. But I have trouble picturing corpses tumbling out of every chair."

"Well, if we took the language of reviews and blurbs seriously, literature would be as lethal as anthrax. You know—*stunning, shattering*—that sort of thing. You'd be a public enemy. But I'm proud of you, Darling. You'll do fine tonight."

"These last few days," Amanda says, sitting beside Hal on the sofa, "I've been feeling like Billy's character, Clark, when I write. My computer screen is like a mirror, and I sit there for hours pushing, pulling, and slapping my experiences into some sort of shape that others will want to look at."

"But Deerling, people *do* look. You've been in magazines, and now a book—a public reading!"

"But it's like in *Morph Man*, when people glance in the window as they pass by, wondering vaguely if that isn't a life-sized ceramic lion crouching on the dinner table, or why the form passing through the dimmed room seemed to have a head equipped with a tuba. Those people are like readers, and my stories are like Clark's hidden selves," she concludes, her voice changing to a parody of melodrama, "and I'm tragically misunderstood. You can't talk me out of it."

"So Billy's book isn't just about himself?"

"It wouldn't be, if it's any good."

"You're a frustrated pharmacist, My Scumptiousness," Hal says. "Why, when I push pills I know that pain will wither and the bugs will get out of Dodge—a lot of the time, anyway. You're right to doubt words. When it comes to rousting suffering and brightening life, the pill is mightier than the pen. Want me to call and cancel for you tonight?"

"Can I use that crap about pills in my next story?"

"Is that all I am, raw material?"

"Sweetie-Darling, that's the fate of your gender. Certainly God couldn't have thought that he finished the job when he invented the male. That story that you guys made up about the rib isn't as bonkers as Billy's mutations, but at least it shows that guys are aware of their incompleteness.

"But seriously," Amanda continues, "don't you think that there's something beyond the reach of chemistry? Don't you think there's a problem in how we've started treating all sorts of moral failures as though they're just medical issues? He abuses children? Give him the blue pill. Beats his wife? The white pill should fix that. We've lost the capacity to make judgments. *Judgmental* is a bad word now."

"Seriously? I don't have a clue. I realize that we're *supposed* to make moral judgments, but the fact is that pills often work better than sermons."

Later, leaving for the reading at St. Scholastica, I picture

Amanda pausing by the front door to stroke Billy's urn. "For luck," she might have thought.

Amanda's reading goes beautifully. People, including your narrator, form a line such as Hal has never seen for ointments and pills; they count cash or write checks, and a reviewer from *Duluth News Tribune* promises that raves will wash across the region within a week. After the reading, in a spirit of celebration, Amanda and Hal determine that tomorrow they will visit the newly refurbished ballroom in the elegant old Congdon Hotel on Superior Street.

Tomorrow arrives with its usual punctuality, and Hal hurries home in the coolness of a late afternoon in May, finding Amanda at the dressing table in the spare bedroom, her personal den of adornment.

"Hey, this isn't *my* Love Machine," Hal exclaims, bending to gaze at her in the mirror. Hal's Amanda, he affirms, has lovely brown hair that curves smoothly to her shoulders. But this Amanda has auburn hair that rises on imagined breezes and swirls about her Grecian features like passion itself. Hal's Love Machine is a natural beauty, whereas this neo-Amanda augments nature with the sundry and secret powders and lotions that make the enhancement of appearance one of the most lucrative industries in America.

"Do you like it?" Amanda asks, catching Hal's eye in the mirror. "Am I competitive with that redhead you introduced me to at Billy's send-off, the babe you've been chasing through Ladies' Unmentionables every chance you get?"

"How did you . . . ?"

"Trade secret, Sweetie-Darling. I snoop to conquer. But answer. Do you like the new me? Am I better than the old Amanda? What's your take on all this artifice?"

“I like the new Amanda. As to the rest of it, I don’t know what to say.”

Hal finds a chair and sits beside Amanda, their eyes meeting in the mirror. On the radio, Bill Evans begins “You Must Believe in Spring,” and Amanda’s eyes widen.

“Imagine, Hal! My mother talked of hearing him at The Village Vanguard when she was young. He’s been gone for over twenty years now, but here he is, a ghost in the gadgetry.”

“It’s an age of miracles,” Hal concedes.

“Well since, miraculously, you don’t know what to say, let me explain that the makeover is deeper than natural beauty. Natural beauty is just an accident. The makeover is slapped on with a brush, but it tells the story of deep longing.”

“I see,” Hal muses. “Every woman a female impersonator.”

“No, Deerling, every woman a Stradivarius—the mystery of the violin is in the varnish, you know, not the wood.”

“Would that woman’s music were always as sweet.”

“Let’s not debate,” she says, her voice shifting to a more practical key. “It’s the new me. Change is the woman’s prerogative. Take it or leave it.”

“I’ll take it, Darling—time and time again.”

The mirror is framed with ornately crafted rosewood like the carved impression of Amanda’s new hair. As “Darlings” and “Deerlings” fill the air like attendant sprites, Hal admires the happy faces that admire him in return, his head listing a bit into Amanda’s auburn swirls.

Parting thoughts. The human character, now a mystery that is too often fashioned by medicine, is like a soap opera. Our thoughts, beliefs, and feelings are actors beneath cranial arches, entering and exiting in an endless to-do. Sometimes a beloved belief will leave the stage forever, banished from the script either by judgment or chemistry, to be replaced by a new performer, who may join the cast bellowing and strutting like a bull or creeping silently like a cat under cover of night. Likewise, a particular feeling may be demoted from a central role to a supporting one. A person's character, like the soap opera, is a drama that is never finished, never, that is, until each of us dons futile wings and makes his final plunge.

Will Amanda and Hal live happily ever after? Will the feelings that constitute their present love remain central to the pageant of their lives? It's needless to say where our hopes lie, but it's impossible to say what scenes will play in that unconstructed theater that we call the future. It's a limitation of stories, but one they share with life itself, that they must always end on this unfinished side of tomorrow.

But while it is still today, Hal and Amanda smile, dab a few tears, and exchange a prodigious assortment of kisses and snuggles. Finally, after much rearranging of hair and garb, they arrive at the front door, where they pause at the oak cabinet to thank the ashes for blessings freely if obscurely rendered. They enjoy an early dinner at the Congdon, then it's tango time.

That, at any rate, is the story, and some of it is true.

Author's note: The mutations depicted in Billy's *Morph Man* were suggested by John Biguenet's story "Gregory's Fate" in *The Torturer's Apprentice* (The Ecco Press, 2001).

The Boy in the Attic

When Tommy was a child there was a story about a crooked man. Everything about the man was crooked. He lived in a crooked house on a crooked road. And so on. That was a long time ago. Tommy was also crooked, but then things went all crooked in his life, too, and he and his father left his mother tangled in a heap with a strange man in the bed in a dilapidated house. It was an old bed, and Tommy would hear it creak and rock like the boat his father took him on once. The tangled heap and the strange man were thanks to drugs, and drugs happened after Tommy's mother had started to be a stripper to keep her weight down.

"Lemme get this straight," his father had said, and then he got the puddles in his eyes.

Then they came north from the big city with the dilapidated house and the creaky bed to this city, Tommy and his father did. But his father only stayed three months because he had a calling. It came on the phone. Leaving is what you do.

Now Tommy is the crooked man. The avenue that he lives on wobbles uphill at a funny angle. Tommy climbs this avenue in the late afternoon, passing the fat lady with her grocery bags. When the old gray house comes into view, it does not stick straight up. The sidewalk to the porch twists and turns through bushes, and the boards of the porch seem to have collided together like pieces in a kaleidoscope. Tommy must be careful climbing the steps to the front door. Like Tommy himself, everything is just a little off.

A little off is what his mother used to say when she didn't feel good.

"I'm just a little off today, Sweetie. Pass Mama that bottle and that pillbox like a good boy."

The staircase also twists and turns, and the ceiling of Tommy's room in the attic slants down toward the outer wall. Only someone as small as Tommy could stand straight up by the window, which Tommy himself cannot do because he is always bent thanks to being born that way almost thirty years ago. If you put your pennies and nickels or your pack of gum on the windowsill they might slide off, because the windowsill tips down like the lip of the man who puts things in bags along with Tommy.

In the early evening, Tommy stands in the window, which looks out into a backyard with trees. Further off, the different avenues are lined with houses, and the avenues and houses are scrambled all the way down to the lake. People tug their shadows up the hill like overcoats, and when fog comes in from the lake the people become ghosts.

Sometimes Tommy walks the different avenues, even when the manager reminds him to go straight home. The manager has a scar on his cheek like a pirate. On Tommy's own avenue is the blue house where he saw an old man crying on his porch. And one day on one of the streets, which go the other way from avenues, Tommy saw a person leave in an ambulance. He had things coming from his nose, and they slid him in the back door of the ambulance like when you slide a stick of gum back into the pack.

Some days Tommy is late, and Aunt Susan scolds and talks about God at dinner as Tommy bends over his bowl and stirs a wreckage of crackers in his tomato soup, or as he squirts a wiggly line of ketchup along his hot dog. The scolding makes him want to go away, which is what you do, and he tries to think where he would go.

Tommy is shaped like an egg—an egg on two toothpicks that certainly are about to break. I'm Humpty Dumpty, Tommy thinks as he stands in front of the mirror before bedtime. He must clean the toothpaste from the mirror or Aunt Susan will scold about that, too. I'm Humpty Dumpty in a nest, Tommy thinks, pulling the sheets to his chin and waiting for sleep. I'm a little Easter Egg, but if I had the right pills I wouldn't be.

The boy who comes in Tommy's store from the Target store told Tommy about the pills. The Target boy had to go away from his mother too. As he goes to sleep, Tommy imagines what he would do with the pills. He would become rubber and pull his body into any shape that he wants. For instance, if the girl he likes drops her keys over the fence, he would make his arm long and thin and get her keys back. Or if she wants to know, standing with Tommy on the sidewalk after work, what they are saying about her inside, Tommy would stretch his ears out as big as a satellite dish and listen for her. And if she says she wants a pet, Tommy would yank himself into the shape of a puppy or turtle. Then she'd smile and put her hands on him like his mother did.

These things happen in his head. The girl works in the part of the store where they bake things, and in another part Tommy puts what the people buy into bags after first saying paper or plastic, which he says better than the man with the windowsill lip. He doesn't know the girl's name. Finally, as he snuggles in his bed, these thoughts go away, turning and turning like water going down.

Sometimes as he goes to sleep, a dark person that Tommy heard about in a story, a person from a far away country where everyone rides camels, comes in the moonlight through Tommy's window to talk about the sadness. He has cloth wrapped around his head and a large coat like a woman's dress, and he tells Tommy that he must keep the sadness inside and not let it hatch. If you let the sadness hatch, people will sew up your lips.

When the story person is there, Tommy says very little. The person sits in the chair by the window where the moonlight falls on him. After warning Tommy not to let the sadness hatch, he gets to the good part. The good part is, if you remember why you are here and do what you are supposed to do, the Great Powers will let you live in a house where the porch is okay and you will have a room with a straight ceiling and a bathroom on the same floor. Oh, and the house won't creak in the dark. Then, seeing the hunger in Tommy's eyes, the person from far away says that, yes, the girl will talk to him too, just like his mother did before she started to lose weight. Tommy smiles, and the dark person finishes by explaining to Tommy what he must remember to do. Then he leaves, dissolving into the moonlight like brown sugar in cream. Then the moon goes away, and the night is as black as Aunt Susan's Bible.

Birds awaken Tommy with their squabbling. Hey fuzz butt, this branch is for robins! No, it's for sparrows! And so on. Tommy laughs to think what they are saying. Then, with the sun bubbling up beyond the trees and the houses and the lake, Tommy is a crooked person in his tilted window watching the birds and further away the whipped-cream clouds that fold themselves together over the lake.

It is early in May. The snow is gone, and Tommy wonders if the mama birds are laying eggs. In the fall they will go south. All down the hill different houses jostle each other, and maybe they squabble like the birds. But we can't hear how houses talk. Above the houses, treetops are hands stroking the sky in the wind. Then, looking down to the ground below his window, Tommy thinks about all the king's horses and all the king's men.

The window is very dirty, and one of the panes is cracked. When Tommy moves back and forth and looks through the different panes the world outside wiggles. He pretends that the dust on the panes makes little scenes from stories and that the crack is a giant hill. He must look through the story scenes to see the real scene outside. And then there are the tiny squiggles like Tinker Toys that float in his eyes. There are many things to see through before you can see.

A man standing on the next avenue, pausing as he walks his own crooked mile, might gaze up past the nearest house, past the trees, and through the dusty attic window where a ghostly shape stands and looks down on him. But the man would not see from such a distance that Tommy's eyes are lost. Certainly he would not see the eyes turn inward in grief and rage as Tommy tries to recall the words of the story person who came at night in the moonlight. Nor would the man on the avenue hear Tommy howl at his inability to remember what he has come here to do. The howl would stay in the attic.

The Celebrated Stripper of Subfusc County

Sometimes, leaning on my mop by the old suit of armor, I'd watch them through the window while I cleaned up in the restaurant. Half the time Homer was late, and it was just Paula and Oscar in the parking lot next to Babe, our sky-blue stork, in the moonlight by the county road. To the naked eye, they didn't match-up real good back then. Oscar only amounts to about five-foot-nine and one-forty. His right knee can't bend thanks to Vietnam, and he gobbled pain pills loose from his pockets—still does. Now Paula, though, she was a different load of beef back then. Everything about Paula was writ in spades, and her walking problems were a matter of payload.

Oscar's what you might call conversationally challenged, and folks joke that he needs a special license plate. In those courting days, I'd try to imagine, standing at the window by Lancelot—we named that rusty heap of armor Lancelot—I'd imagine Oscar's "yups" and "nopes" out there struggling to do romantic duty as he'd stare down at the gravel with the bats swooping overhead. From time to time he'd tip his head way back to look at Paula above the bosoms, which some folks referred to as the Alps.

And sometimes I'd get a tear in my eye from remembering about me and Irene when we were young, and how we had wished the stork would land on our porch. It's strange how sometimes a memory can be soft and nice, and other times that same memory can feel like a swallowed stone. And often the memory of Irene would swoop from one to the other, from softness to hurt, just like those bats in the parking lot as I'd stand there with my mop and bucket at the restaurant window.

Like I said, Paula was a big fat woman, six-foot-two and boo-coo pounds. If Paula took a notion to go calling, Homer, that's her brother, he'd hoist her into the back of the 4x4 and check the tires. Homer's a big man himself, strong as an ox, some say, and twice as smart. Paula is a patriot, and when they started talking on the TV news about how Americans better lose weight, and also when she saw how businesses in the county were suffering from the effects of the flood, well, Paula, she put two and two together and came up with the idea to be a stripper.

"Say what?" Homer asked.

Paula explained how stripping would trim the fat and raise public awareness, but Homer, who works at the paper mill down in Black Paw, he replied how he didn't want to think of other things that might rise if guys from the mill were gawking at her shaking her booty like Jello. He was proud of that remark and repeated it to all the boys at the barbershop, stretching his grin around a row of gravestones that pass for teeth.

"And besides," Homer told her, "you can't dance a lick that I ever seen. Strippers gotta dance, you know. It ain't just standing there strugglin' out of them bib overalls."

But Paula was determined, and this is how me and my friend Ole fit in. There had been hard times up where I worked on the Mesabi Iron Range, still are. There's folks up there happy to eat crow soup, and that ain't just an expression. Anyway, after Irene passed away I lost my job, and that little split-entry house where we had lived together all those years became a haunted place. So I packed up some stuff, sold the house, and moved down here to Cold Beak.

I wasn't sure what I'd do with myself here, but pretty quick Providence showed up disguised as a defunct fried chicken place for sale on the county road out by I 35, not far from where the New Hope River winds through our valley and makes it so pretty, nothing like what you might think just hearing a name like Cold

Beak. Me and Ole, we figured we know a business opportunity when it puts its paws on your chest and licks your face, and we snapped that old chicken place right up.

So we set to fixing it into a fancy supper club with lots of red felt and mirrors to cover where the windows were boarded. It was good, after all that sadness up on the Range, to be building something. Ole and me sang and sawed and hammered away, pausing at noon to unwrap sandwiches and pickles, which we ate quick so's they wouldn't get saw dust and plaster on them, then plunging back into creativity, which uninformed folks might have called mayhem. Ole even had the idea to paint pictures on the ceiling, like in that church that you hear about in Italy, but we finally figured we'd best let that dog rest.

One afternoon, it was May and the weather had just turned warm, we were outside figurin' where to put the plaster stork as we waited for Lars Johnson, the plumber, to show his bony face. Lars had vowed to make every effort to be there that day, "every effort" being the workman's escape clause—the fine print in the verbal agreement. There's people that say Lars ain't worth the dynamite it takes to wake him up, but I say he's okay once he gets to gettin'.

Oscar, who's my younger brother, was there that day pretending to help when Homer pulled up in his Dodge Ram with Paula as cargo in a big cushioned chair. It was like she was the Queen of Mardi Gras up there with her blond curls popping out in all directions like bed springs. Hauling Paula down onto solid ground wasn't something you undertook just for small talk, so me and Ole and Oscar walked on over so she could stay put. The saplings that we had planted off to one side of the parking lot leaned on their crutches and gawked at the show.

"See you got that plaster stork you was talkin' about," Homer observed, climbing out of the cab. Homer had a voice full of rumblings and explosions that would cause a stranger to take a step back and check for exits.

"Yes sir!" Ole beamed, unphased by Homer's volume. "New

owner of that miniature golf place up in Hinckley couldn't see no use for it, so I got her for a song. Good as new, too, 'cept for where kids splashed paint on her butt there."

"Well, you get her painted up," Homer predicted, "and she's gonna look real good. You fixin' to call this place The Stork Club then?"

"We ain't decided on a name yet," Ole said, "but I figure a supper club can always benefit by a stork, whatever you name it." Eventually we called the club The County Road Vista to avoid confusion.

In this part of the country there's always some introductory thrashing around the bush, and if there's no stork handy you can always talk about the weather, which we did for a while too that breezy day in May when the Paula float pulled up. But finally Paula said how she hadn't got all afternoon to be the big attraction in the back of a pickup, and so we were "cutting to the chase." She liked to talk like city folks on television.

The chase was how Paula wanted me and Ole to let her strip in our plush new supper club. She took her a pinch of snoose—what folks from elsewhere call snuff—and focused her eyes down at us from her throne, eyes big as moons under that curly, springy hair. Then she explained how we boys had the opportunity to be part of history because this wouldn't be the sort of strip club that exploits poor young girls that can't find a decent job. This would be a strip club that would help fat people have pride while they trim themselves down. The way Paula explained it, you can try to improve without being ashamed of yourself in the meantime.

We were all pretty quiet for a moment after Paula's declaration, and she just sat there on her throne giving us the doe-eye. You could of heard a moth fart. Ole adjusted his feed cap and stared off at some clouds over the Mobile station, and Oscar found a few stones to push around with his sneaker. If Oscar was in Cold Beak to court his old flame, which we all figured he was, he was doing a darn pokey job stoking up his nerve. Folks were always making chances for him to throw light on the issue of him and Paula, but

Oscar isn't much for throwing light. He's more your fog chucker. Anyway, pretty quick Paula went on about how she pictured it all.

"The way I picture it all, we gotta divide that club in two. Folks don't want to be eatin' their meat and potatoes with a big ol' fat girl yankin' her clothes off and shaken her stuff right there. They don't want their kids askin' a bunch of questions. So the strip club is a separate room, where we serve drinks and carrot sticks with low-fat dip."

"And besides," Homer put in, dropping his elephant's trunk of an arm over the door of the cab, doing his beaver grin, and lowering his voice so's the folks inside the Mobile station wouldn't hear, "we're gonna put shock absorbers under that stage so there ain't no tidal waves in the beverages next door."

"I got this stage name picked out," Paula continued, ignoring her brother, whose fat jokes were wearing thinner each year, "and it's Paullota, because there's a lotta me. We have this big horse scale on the stage, and folks can buy chances on the day when I get me down to 300. On that day I change my name to Paulessa, and someone wins the jackpot. What you think of my idea, Oscar?" she finished off, homing in on my brother dead in the eye.

Oscar, he had no more to say than a minnow in a pond, and the clouds over the Mobile station were still pretty interesting to Ole. I expected him to say how they looked like this animal or that. Oscar was back to pushing his shoe around in the gravel, and my own fingernails grew an inch before Ole spoke up.

"Well," Ole said, jerking his eyes down from the stratosphere, "you sure got you a new idea there, Paula, and we're gonna give it serious thought. I never did make a business decision straight off the bat, and there's lots of sides we gotta look at. Like whether the community is ready for such . . . things. But we're gonna think on it and then we'll get back to you." Then he tugged at the beak of that old feed cap as if something formal was going on.

"Might as well surrender right now, boys," Homer bellowed as he climbed back into the cab. "Arguing with Paula is like arguing with cement."

He jammed the pickup into reverse, nearly colliding with an old van labeled Johnson Plumbing that Lars's "every effort" (and that mythical stick of dynamite) had brought to our driveway. Of course no plumbing work actually occurred that day. It was just the warm-up visit, the one where the workman walks around, nods wisely, and spouts terminology. He'd get started in a few days, he said. Up in these parts, you can sometimes tell from a fellow's rocking hand just how broad a term "a few days" is meant to be. The rocking of Lars's hand made it clear that nothing was clear.

Now this might be the point in the story where I ought to stick in some sort of villain, someone that can be described real vivid, maybe with skin like grease bubbling in the pan who never takes a bath and who's out to thwart Paula. But this isn't a made-up story for a book. Maybe it'll get to be a story like that when folks in future generations here in Subfusc County tell about Paula. Maybe this made-up guy with the skin problem—I see him with a cigarette poking out of one side of his mouth and his breath whistling in the other—will have secret, whiskey-soaked meetings out in the woods with his cohorts, and maybe there'll be a plot to burn down the new restaurant. Or, since everything's got its shadow, maybe tomorrow's storytellers will make Paula's enemy be another woman like the ones we ogled in the *Zapp Comics* years ago.

From a storytelling point of view, I can see how having a villain would make sense and come to be, just as dreaming up Judas made story sense by puttin' flesh and blood on the idea of betrayal. But the truth is that the villain in Cold Beak was just the circumstances themselves—the bad economy, the old attitudes that people clung to, and other vague stuff that really wasn't wrapped up in any one person.

Of course there was debate and falderal about Paula's plan. The churches in town, Ole said, acted like branches of one religion called Judgmentalism. And Old Lady Emerson said some pretty rude things. She's one of those who never had a thought blow through her head that she didn't straightway express—one of those that only see the meanness inside themselves but think that it's in the world outside, like thinking the air is full of insects when it's just floaters in your eyes. One time me and Ole tried to dream up a situation where you wouldn't mind being alone with Elvira Emerson. Ole, he came up with being crash-landed on a glacier with the campfire dying and the other food already eaten.

Anyway, once Paula promised that she wouldn't take *everything* off, that there would be a costume with spangles and feathers and safety pins big as shoes for the grand finale, well, once that was cleared up it was the Chamber of Commerce that carried the day by convincing folks of the potential economic advantage to Cold Beak and all of Subfusc County. Next thing you know *The Weekly Peep* had a front page article celebrating the whole idea and giving me and Ole a bunch of attaboys for hosting the Paula "concept" in our super club.

And darned if the Chamber and *The Peep* weren't right, and Homer was right too about not arguing with cement. He's really a bunch smarter than an ox. The grand opening of the County Road Vista and the Paula Show was on the Fourth of July, just a few days after Lars, following a medley of worried phone calls, got the plumbing done. People came in bus loads all the way down from Duluth and over from New Persiflage, and further off too. The motel was jammed full, and Barry Olson let out plots for campers in a field where he forgot to plant his soybeans. The line at the Vista straggled out past the stork, and Marvin Updahl, he's our Sheriff, Marvin sent one of his boys to patrol the crowd so's they wouldn't spill into traffic.

You can tell from the polished shoes when folks ain't from around here, and the group from Houston had neckties big as sandwich boards. We sat them down at the table by Lancelot, the suit of armor Ole found down in St. Paul. Lancelot is sort of propped up with sticks inside, but his ax is always poised for trouble. The Texans were "crapulous and carminative, in that order," Ole said, who had got himself a vocabulary book so as to impress bigwigs coming to see Paula. We figured if there was any ghost in that armor capable of judgment, the ax might see some use. The Texans only stayed in Cold Beak a day, though, not brushing too close to any of us hayseeds, maybe figuring that the snoose habit would rub off and next thing you know they'd be smooching with farm animals.

And I suppose—since we're coming to the part of the story where the villain, if there was one, would be booed and carried out of town on a rail—I suppose when folks in the future tell the Paula story, there might be a temptation to stick in villainous tourists like extra jokers in the deck. They might tell it so's the Texans come to town and just out of old ranch-style meanness find ways to try to undo all the good that Paula was doing for Cold Beak. Because to tell the truth, people here in Cold Beak are a little insecure about outsiders, afraid they'll think that we're just a bunch of doofusses. And lots of times in stories villains are stirred up out of such fears. But the Texans didn't really do any harm, and most of the tourists seemed pretty darned friendly.

If you can call your kid brother a tourist, Oscar was the most regular of the tourists, dragging his shrapneled leg around in Paula's wake. He was nervous at first on account of he hadn't seen many near-naked women outside the family, if the family includes the cousins over in Frog Landing. But coming to view Paula was a publicized event, like seeing the Gophers play the Badgers, not a guilty, sneak-around event. So shyness melted right off like frost on the windshield.

Paula called what she did "performance pieces," and there was one at eight and one at ten Wednesday through Saturday. She worked hard, her blond curls flapping, and each night a few pounds melted straight down her legs and through the cracks in the floor. Paula waved various props around—bacon strips, cheese wheels, frying pans, and so on—and every now and then she'd yank off some piece of clothing. Jan Tollerud, sitting at the end of the bar under the antlers, gawked so hard that a fly buzzed into his mouth and out again a minute later. Jan is always disheveled and pungent, like he's been rolled in kitty litter, and there are those who wonder if he was formed by human contact.

One night Paula tugged a live piglet from her smock. It escaped squealing over the bar, knocking the carrot dip into the lap of the art critic who was up from Minneapolis. The pig hid behind the juke box for the rest of the evening, letting out a little oink now and then as it saw fit. But the critic gave Paula a good write-up anyway. He saw lots of meaning that us folks in Cold Beak couldn't see, and his review was full of words like "sudorific" and "postmodern." That quieted the last of Paula's detractors, and from then on, in her finale costume, she was Queen Paula, our laughing, dancing savior.

When Paula started her book, that Paglia woman came from Harvard to help with the spelling and stuff. She was nice. Me and her went fishing, and she even caught a perch. Thousands of copies of the book were sold on the Internet, and when Paula went on Oprah some doctors from St. Paul called about opening a fat farm under her name. Quick as you can grill a bratwurst, they built a hotel-type place out on the New Hope River by the old creamery. But just as quick, it started to sink into the river, what with the weight of all the clients. It was like the river was saying that it had its own job and wanted to be left alone. But Barry Olson sold them that field that had been the camp ground, and now we have the Paula Pringle Institute, with its famous Rotunda of Resolve, raking in the dollars on high ground, looking down on the river and the new golf course.

So Paula saved Cold Beak after the flood. She shook and shimmied and laughed until God winked down on Subfusc County and the whole region was prosperous and smiling. Everyone in town lined up at the bank with piles of bills to be counted out with much licking of thumbs. The collection plates are still stuffed every Sunday, and the Judgmentalists have let their outrage evaporate like last year's joke. Why, I even saw the husband of one of the pastors wearing a Paula sweatshirt in the grocery store the other day. Seems like a moral position don't have much chance against prosperity, a carton of milk's got more shelf life. I thought that up and said it to the boys at the barbershop and they laughed, except for Jan, who's about as dumb as a box of rocks.

By-and-by Paulotta got to be Paulessa and plunked for matrimony. After a few months of courting in the moonlight by the stork, with the bats scribbling their swoops in the air overhead and me looking through the window, Oscar shuffled off with his bride back to his little farm south of here. That's where they live now, and they have me down to supper Sundays when I'm not busy at the County Road Vista. And I hear that there are a lot of fat people marrying up at the Pringle Institute, which doubles as a weight-loss clinic and a love boat. The local clergy got themselves new cars and new sun decks on their houses thanks to the spike in the bliss business. Seems like everyone's getting married except Ole and me.

Homer, he moped for a month or two when he didn't have his sister to haul around, but then he started stretching himself out in the new tanning salon. He got brown and shiny as a Thanksgiving turkey, then he took to splashing on cologne, tugging on his Paula sweatshirt, and walking the road up by the Institute. Folks thought he was climbing a fool's hill, but darned if he ain't gonna be married next month. We're not an adventuresome people here in Subfusc County, and one of the boys at the barbershop commented on the wisdom of Homer picking a fat gal.

"It's like with ice cream," the fellow said. "Once you get used to a flavor, ain't no sense in changing."

"Or it's like when you got a good fishing hole," Jan Tollerud put in, shooing a fly off his nose. "No point drivin' up every dirt road lookin' for another."

A third fellow was about to offer his comparison, but Homer roared out, flashing his rubble of teeth so's they'd know he wasn't mad, that any more such talk wouldn't be polite. Usually talking about good taste with the boys at the shop is about as productive as discussing the Dow with a carload of basset hounds. But when a big man like Homer asks for quiet in a voice that rips cobwebs and knocks the sparrow dirt off rafters, folks don't get analytical. So, as cuttings accumulated on the floor and pomade penetrated scalps, the boys took to boasting about fish they'd caught and people they'd met, all lies and tall tales shameful enough to shrivel the ears.

One Sunday in October I was down to the farm for Paula's special meatloaf supper. The day was warm for the time of year, so before eating we sat in the yard and watched the swallows arcing about. The creek in back of the house, which empties into the New Hope River about a mile away, made a soft sound. The maple leaves in the grass were sheets of gold beat thin, the sunset was all purple and orange, and the clouds on the horizon had that corrugated look. People's spit was all bronze from the snoose, and their remarks seemed poetic and beautiful, no matter what they really said.

We watched the cattle out in the pasture shuffling back toward their dormitory, pulling their shadows along. Pretty soon Oscar would be hooking up the milking machines. In the meantime, smiling sheepishly off toward the corncrib, he performed an overture of throat clearing. Then he asked if I wanted a nephew or a niece. Paula's under 200 now, and the doctor thinks everything will be smooth as butter.

Me and Ole, we've been sharing the same house for quite a while. We added a room on the back for the pool table and the Paula memorabilia, and Lars Johnson, after every effort, found time to fix us up with a sauna and a hot tub. And I've got my pictures of Irene. It was hard losing her, and, as I said, hard when jobs dried up on the Iron Range. There was folks up there, and for a while I was one of them, who just wanted to crawl under the ground and pull it over them.

Now that I'm where the economy is better, thanks to Paula,

I wonder how Irene would feel if I started walking up by the Institute like Homer did so's I could meet me one of them prosperous types too. It's been a lovely sight, seeing people all rich and fat ambling along the road when the air is snappy and the leaves turn color. But I guess it's like what that fellow at the barbershop said about ice cream—Irene was the best gift to my life, and experiments would be ungrateful. And besides, Irene is doin' a pretty good imitation of a river, waltzing and laughing through my thoughts and making a summertime sound. I wouldn't change it.

It's winter now in the real world. A couple months ago, me and Ole got us a big St. Bernard named Swede, who drips saliva by the quart and snacks on the evening newspaper. On a cold night there's nothing like stretching out by the fireplace with Swede and some cocoa in my Paula mug. Then I think about Oscar and Paula, and also about rusty old Lancelot and Babe, our sky-blue stork. Soon I turn to thinking how I'll be playing with my nieces and nephews and wondering what new wrinkles they'll give the world by-and-by.

If you ask me, there's a lot of fine things still ahead in Cold Beak. When I try to imagine them as I relax in the evening, they mix themselves up with thoughts of Irene when we were young and starting out on the Range. And all those hopes and memories, the personal things and the things about Cold Beak, and America too, and the future—all those things are a river laughing and turning in my head while Swede dozes, digesting the evening news and turning all of the world's troubles into fertilizer. And then it seems to me that the embers in the fireplace are a city that you see at night coming over a hill in your car, a city down in a valley glowing with dreams, a cluster of separate dreams that add up to one big dream.

The Last Bijou

Andre loves the Vieux Carre. It's delightful to lie in bed on Saturday night, safe behind burglar bars, savoring the call of trombones, trumpets, and clarinets drifting from the open doors of Bourbon Street's Dixieland clubs—a gumbo of tempos and tunes spiced with shattering glass, shouts, and maybe a gunshot or siren. Then, as the din from the Quarter fades in waves, Andre dreams of the house on Chestnut Street, where as a child he sat cross-legged with his sister on the living room floor as Mom brought mountainous bowls of popcorn and they watched Spike Jones and His City Slickers on Milton Berle.

When the lights go up on a Sunday morning, Andre, loosed from his dreams, dons his red beret and steps out onto the Quarter's stage, marshaling an appetite for coffee and a pastry at the Croissant d'Or. If the street cleaning has been delayed, Andre loves to breathe the scent of urine and stale beer, to bask in the panorama of abandoned Lucky Dogs like miniature logs, regurgitated oysters, and discarded napkins stained with the various coagulated residues of vice, gluttony, and disease. It is thrilling to be a connoisseur of decadence amid smashed bottles, crumpled wrappers and bags, an occasional needle, a tampon, and blood stains on a wall. Crossing Bourbon Street, he gazes down the vanishing row of jazz clubs and saloons, the bespattered street stretching away like a mammoth slab of pizza with all the toppings. Always in Andre's mind there is music, an orchestra in the pit or a juke box in the corner, and as he turns toward

Ursulines Street his insides swell with the strains of *Oh What a Beautiful Morning.* Certainly something wonderful is coming his way!

At the Croissant d'Or, he lingers over his choice from the exquisite cast of fresh pastries displayed behind glass, each type separated from the others like cliques at a party—almond croissants, chocolate croissants, croissants dusted with sugar, brioches the size of hats, éclairs snoozing in their chocolate blankets, portly Danishes stuffed with an array of fillings, trays of variously concocted muffins, a banana bread to die for, something with crumbs sparkling on the outside and mush of peach inside, and even long-gone childhood's favorite, the incomparable, corpulent cream puff, ready to ooze at the first bite.

The pudgy lady behind the pastries has served him often, though not so often as his mother. She is usually patient like Mom was, unless, as sometimes happens, a hungry crowd behind him resorts to muttering.

And how thrilling to play the man of leisure on the patio by the marble fountain with its lilies and goldfish, a fresh bouquet on the table, with French roast coffee, a chocolate croissant or cream puff, and the Sunday *Times-Picayune.* He reads of public officials and their latest scams, of David Duke throwing his hood in the ring again, and of golfers shooting birdies and pars. After the anti-climactic funnies, he steps out again onto Ursulines, the pavement steaming after a morning shower, when the last raindrops are children on holiday skipping down the street. He admires the buildings that are like the stubby, exposed ganglia of something huge and maimed, something opened to the sun that is quickly dispatching the remaining clouds like so much lint. Oh what a beautiful morning!

He strolls to the flea market to muse among costumes and props of past lives, to finger faded shirts, cracked cups and saucers, and vinyl records in disintegrating jackets. Perhaps a music lover has died, and Andre imagines a deathbed scene where a loved one places a favorite album beneath the needle of an ancient stereo for the last time. Sometimes Andre buys an album, maybe one of Frank Sinatra with a jaunty hat and one arm raised in the body language of song, or of Doris Day gazing at a sunset, or maybe Joan Baez barefoot with her guitar at Big Sur. For half an hour each Sunday, he is an archeologist of life's dreams, brooding over tables of tools and artifacts, sensing the mystery of others' stories, hearing their soft, sad melodies.

Soon it is time to walk the center aisle of the Farmers Market, to talk with bucolic venders about oranges, to inquire about grapefruit and peaches. Examining the produce displayed in long tables on either side of the aisle, he hears in his mind Rosemary Clooney's song about lovely bunches of coconuts. Many of the venders know him by sight and call to him until he settles on his choice of fruit for the bench by the river, and this time for Mom as well.

Next he passes the Café du Monde, jammed with tourists eating beignets and rubbing powdered sugar from sleeves and shirt fronts before they head out with cameras and children dangling, perhaps to ride in one of the many donkey-drawn carriages that wait by Jackson Square.

Andre notices a familiar carriage and crosses Decatur to say hello. He often takes Leon's tour of the Quarter, enjoying to hear again the history of the Cabildo, the Old Mint, and the Ursulines Convent. Although Leon speaks the mainstream dialect, Andre hears him in the black dialect of old movies, and later Andre remembers bows and shuffles that hadn't been.

"How's business, Leon?"

"It be berry good Mr. Bijou, sir. And how is you? I sees you doan got yo camera t'day."

"My camera's being repaired, Leon. Other than that I'm tip-top, thank you. Tell me, because I can never remember, is your trusty steed a donkey or a mule?"

"This one be a mule, Mr. Bijou."

"And what exactly is the difference between a donkey and a mule?"

"Well, sir, a mule it come from matin' a ass wid a horse, and a mule doan make no other mule—he what you call sterile."

"I see. Miscegenation, Leon. Let that be a warning. By the way, does it have to be a male ass and a female horse, or can it be the other way around?"

"No sir, Mr. Bijou. No other way 'round. It always got to be a boy ass an' a girl horse. Dat fo' sho'."

"But mules themselves can be either sterile boy mules or sterile girl mules?"

"Well, I reckon dey can, but dey doan pay each other no never mind. No sir."

"Well, I'm sure your mule has a good life. He must enjoy taking people around the Vieux Carre."

"He get plenty hay an' water. But as to enjoyin' . . . well, he just a mule, Mr. Bijou. He just turn de same corner ev'y day."

"In that case, I hope that you at least enjoy your day, Leon. Thank you for sharing your barnyard biology. Every day is an education."

"An' de berry same to you, Mr. Bijou."

Andre crosses the street and climbs the steps to the top of the levee, away from the turbulence of tourists eddying about balloon-twisting mimes, street musicians, and panhandlers. There is time before the second Mass in the St. Louis Cathedral to sit on his usual bench and meditate.

Two young men in pastel colors wander by, discussing a recent evening:

"So just as this gorgeous cruiser strolls through the door, Allen lifts Jeffery's wig right off of his knobby head and slam-dunks it in a puddle on the bar!"

"And I hear the cruiser was a real hottey."

"Sweetheart, trust me, you needed oven mitts. I'm told Allen has new blisters to prove it."

Andre thinks about Mom as his hand gropes in the bag from the Farmers Market. There is just time for a peach, which he eats while admiring a pink smear of abandoned bubble gum on the walkway. Two yards further off a pigeon is eating pizza. Do they still have those nuggets of Double Bubble, he wonders, with the paper twisted on both sides of the savory cargo? Or is the gum always a slab now, next to some absurd baseball cards? Minutes pass. Then, as he stands, he sees on the branch of a crepe myrtle the trembling wings of a bronze butterfly asleep in the lavender shade.

The walk past Jackson Square to the St. Louis Cathedral is cluttered today with all of Indiana, corn-fed folks with voices chippered-up for vacation, and with all of Tokyo, well-cameraed people with sing-song voices and skin the color of French fries.

After the Mass, a stroll to Canal Street to catch the streetcar, to enjoy the rattle and sway up St. Charles Avenue to Foucher. Peering out the window, Andre is joyously in the center of a Spike Jones production of *Clang, Clang, Clang Went the Trolley*, a drama of Buicks and Pontiacs and Toyotas stopping and swerving, snagging at intersections, left-turning and right-turning, all stuffed with people on their way to Sunday visits, to an early afternoon movie, to cheer Jimmy's softball team, or to cruise the shops in the Riverwalk. Smiling, he remembers his father's Ford, unused and dusty now in the garage, still bearing the license plate that reads DR WHIZ.

Then the walk to Touro Infirmary, where Mom, who once starred at the Southern Rep, plays her final scene. She is bivouacked among the usual accessories of disease, and today Andre finds that tubes have been added, tubes coming from her nose like long noodles of snot. They're for oxygen, Nurse Wilfred explains before continuing her rounds of mercy. The dozen roses that Andre sent keep silent vigil on the nightstand. As he inhales their fragrance, Mom's hand struggles heroically with bedding and tubing, emerging at last to where he can fondle her ancient knuckles as duty and affection dictate. He snatches the red beret from his head and perches on the edge of the bed, feet dangling above the floor like pendants. He takes her hand and fumbles in the pungent silence for a topic.

"Mom," he finally asks, "remember when Grandma died? They used oxygen tents then, and the first time you took me to see her I thought that she was trapped in a big bubble of goo. Remember?"

Her face scrunches, perhaps into a smile. He continues:

"And the way she was propped at that odd angle and doing those funny things with her eyebrows, she looked just like that William F. Buckley guy you and Dad always admired! We could have put her in a talent show right there in the hospital, and she would have won hands down—Buckley-in-a-Bag! Then, when she'd pout, she looked like a little fishy in a baggy ready to come home from the pet store. But I don't know what you look like with all your tubes. Maybe like an oyster served with spaghetti . . . or pasta. I wish I had my camera so I could take a picture of myself beside you!"

She gurgles appreciatively, until a bubble grows from around the noodle in one nostril. Andre weighs her gnarled hand in his, not knowing what to say, watching Mom's nose through many eruptive cycles. It is time for words of love and consolation, time to return ancient favors, nose-wiping favors and everything-will-be-all-right favors.

"It's okay, Mom. You've had a good life, and now you're gurgling and melting. But the docs here at Touro will do their best. I'm going to talk to Doc Melville, ask him to slip something into your I.V. to sort of grease the slide, so to speak. Sort of speed things up. No fun just lingering in the noodles, right? And I called Bultman Funeral Home. I told them that it's two outs and two strikes in the bottom of the ninth. And guess what? They're ready anytime. How's that for service? And I got Benny—remember Benny, who wrote the poem when the car dealer's race horse died? I got Benny to write a eulogy. So don't worry. I'll say Benny's eulogy, then whoosh! Mom Among the Noodles is Ashes in an Urn. It's truly amazing!"

He feels like an actor who has barged into the wrong play, but it is too late to stop. He shifts his weight, still clutching the hand.

"And then you've got eternity. Just think of it, blessed eternity! Do you know how long that is? Have you heard the one about the bird carrying one grain of sand to the moon—no, make it the far side of Andromeda? By the time he gets all the sand in the world up there, eternity is still a party waiting to happen. Do you know how much sand there is? Think hacky-sacks. Think beaches and bunkers. Nevada and New Mexico! And all that time is yours! With nothing to do! You'll just sit there like the head official in tennis and look down on all the future. You'll know what incredible things people think thousands of years from now. How they like their eggs. Will it still be Protestants vs. Catholics, Tulane vs. LSU? You'll know all of the mysteries of space and time—like, do they have Martin Luther King Day in foreign galaxies?

"Now stop blowing bubbles like that, Mom. I know you're excited, and as I said, I'll talk to Doc Melville, slip him a twenty for alacrity—for wings for my angel! Because you have been an angel, Mom, and next time you go to sleep, you might wake up flapping feathers right along with that little bird. Maybe you'll even get to carry a grain of sand!"

Then, placing her hand in the bedding and stroking her head, he adds, "Still, you better fix your hair. There might be reincarnation."

With her tubes and her hair in tangles, with the bedding rumpled, her small face, pale and pocked, is like a Maxfli in the rough. He remembers the peaches.

"By the way, Mom" he says, bringing her back from a distant shore, "I brought you some peaches, but it looks like they drip everything into you now, so I'll just leave one here on the night stand by the roses as a symbol. Unless you want me to mush it up and put it in your I.V. bag? No? Well then, I'm off. What's that? Your swan song's kind of slurred. You're just snorting away at the gates of hog heaven. But if you could talk, I bet you could tell some stories now—or soon!"

He slides off of the bed and places his ear close to her scrunching face.

"Oh that's all right, Mom. Think nothing of it. Kiss, kiss, you old slugabed you."

I'm truly insane, he thinks as he walks down the corridor toward the elevator, appreciating the smell of medicines and chemicals, the sweet scent of doctoring. Hanging like a gargoyle on the side of the bed, he had babbled about cremation and eternity. Truly insane, but Mom understands.

He dodges traffic across Prytania, still clutching his beret, to linger over lunch at the Bluebird Café. At the oyster bar in the rear of the dining room, a young man in an apron pries the crusty shells apart and arranges them on plastic trays, where the shivering oysters await death by stomach acid. In the ashtray on his own table, a half-smoked Virginia Slim, crushed and crumpled, languishes like a cripple in a doorway. Andre wonders if the smoker was a sleek, fast-lane type out of the ads. Or an uptown matron of much rouge and girth. Perhaps a desperate boy in drag. Like Keats's urn, the ashtray won't tell. Then, drifting among his neurons, an old song about foolish things rises to consciousness, even though the cigarette that bears lipstick traces reminds Andre of no one.

The waitress cleans the ashtray, wiping the song away as well. Then Andre savors the day's single glass of chardonnay, a small salad with Italian dressing, and a blackened breast of chicken garnished with parsley and a lemon slice. He muses long over coffee. A woman Andre remembers from the neighborhood branch of the Hibernia Bank enters with her flashing emerald eyes and hair red as a sports car. Andre looks away, then leaves to catch the streetcar on St. Charles back to the Vieux Carre.

The streetcar jostles up memories of childhood in the family house in the Garden District. There was hide-and-seek in the tropical yards and gardens, and, in the evening nestled by his mother's side, there was storybook time. The days rolled by like brightly painted figures on a merry-go-round. Then, as a young adult, he had longed for his childhood, for the coloring books and the songs of school, for the romps under the sprinkler in nothing but his underwear. But longing has ceased its bittersweet crawl beneath the skin, and nostalgia isn't what it used to be. Now his childhood friends have all run off to hide in their grown-up careers, families, and distant homes, and Andre is still "It."

Last week, before her speech became swamped in mucus for her final curtain call, Mom had made him promise to move back to the family house. Years ago, when Andre had already passed the age at which other young men were earning incomes and starting families, Dad, himself a wealthy urologist, had insisted that Andre take his own apartment, that he "learn to connect with the world." Often Dad would become angry, shouting, "Normal up, Buddy!" The issue had been marriage, and Andre remembers Dad's counsel, offered as they waited for the green to clear on the fourth fairway at Lakewood Country Club:

"Don't be ashamed to trade your wealth for beauty, my boy. Guilt and fine sentiments are thugs out to mug the genes. A woman's beauty guarantees reproductive health, and reproductive health cooks the goose of Death. So check her teeth, the curve of her thighs and ass. Check her hips and hooters. You want a babe who'll throw good pups. And remember, Buddy, the eyes are windows to the sinuses. Now step back, boy, and let Dr. Whiz show you how to knock down a six iron into the wind."

Dad had called him Buddy in the early days, before he switched from supporting actor to chief critic of Andre's life, before he made Andre feel that everything he did was done wrong. Even now Andre often wonders if he is holding his fork or tying his shoe correctly. On the rainy night before Dad died in the front bedroom, the oak tree had rapped its old knuckles against the house like some gnarled and ghastly messenger. The life in Dad's eyes had gone dull and vague, like something looking at you through murky water. But for a moment that night the something came closer to the surface, and Dad told Andre that he must eventually come back to be the last Bijou to live in the house on Chestnut Street. And still, in dreams, Andre's father lectures down at him, his huge eyebrows in constant motion over the pools of his eyes like branches in the wind.

Now, as the streetcar sways down St. Charles Avenue, Andre sees that his return to the family house is coming to pass. Looking out of the window at an opal smear of clouds in the sky, he imagines his father's soul ejaculated from his body at the moment of death, ejected like a terrified pilot, only to settle under a billowing chute onto eternal fairways where all the lies are good, all the bunkers are raked, and the duffers never slow you down.

Andre knows, as the streetcar clatters past the Pontchartrain Hotel, that he will miss the Quarter. But Commander's Palace is near the house on Chestnut, and Magazine Street is reputed to have some new restaurants that will do nicely for everyday. And he will be able to keep a dog, perhaps the Alsatian that he had been denied as a child. Yes, the house on Chestnut Street, with its giant white columns that had been painted every spring, its great wrought iron fence filled with arabesques and pirouettes, its curving brick driveway, its ancient oak, its crepe myrtles, and its rose bushes and azaleas—the house will do just fine. And the weeks will continue their gentle loops from Sunday to Sunday.

To his left in the distance, as the streetcar approaches Lee Circle, he sees the Superdome, a mammoth skull (or is it a testicle?) erupting from beneath the city. In a few minutes, exiting the streetcar at Canal Street, he meanders among bars and restaurants that populate the way back to the St. Louis Cathedral. He loves the tranquility of the cathedral, whispering its eternal *holy-oly-oaks in free* amid the noise and clutter of the Quarter, and he sits alone in its coolness, his beret resting on his knee, his rosary cycling slowly through a small hand. As the beads slip through his fingers, he imagines *Ave Maria* sung by Frank Patterson, the tenor voice floating like Spanish moss among Andre's thoughts of his impending role, the Garden District Gentleman. He is about to become the last Bijou.

His younger sister, Ruby, died several years ago in a flaming car wreck, just three months after her breast implants. Andre thought at the time that it was a great risk to your health to alter yourself that way, and what if the new boobs poked someone's eye out? Perhaps Dow-Corning had implanted napalm left over from Vietnam, making Ruby burst into flame during heavy petting at seventy miles per hour. Now Mom's soul is about to rise to heaven like smoke. Now Ruby, Dad, and Mom will nestle in their alabaster jugs, arranged in a row on the mantel beneath the portrait of Grandfather Bijou in the house on Chestnut Street. He imagines shaking the jugs on quiet nights, hearing them whisper inside.

Outside the cathedral, some of the artists who set up camp around Jackson Square each morning are packing their things, although tourists and sunlight remain in abundance. Mary, from whom Andre has purchased many charcoal drawings, is one of those calling it a day. Her auburn hair falls softly, like rain, toward the sidewalk as she bends to gather and fold the paraphernalia of the street artist. He will enter offering fruit.

"Good afternoon, Mary. You look rosy today. Would you care for a peach?"

"Peaches today? Thanks, Mr. B. You and your fruit are as inevitable as baseball scores this summer. By the way, how is your mother?"

"Putting on the eighteenth green," Andre says, making a sad, philosophical smile. "What about you? Have you made a solid day's worth of likenesses?"

"Likeness-wise, it's been a swell day, Mr. B," she replies, running fingers through her great festoonery of hair.

"I enjoy glancing up at the wall to see my own likeness, especially those you've made. It's comforting to have one's likeness about the house . . . a sort of verification. But tell me, Mary, why are we so excited about a charcoal and pastel drawing made by a single hand? Why are these more prized than snapshots, which are also remarkable things? Centuries of science and genius have gone into the evolution of the camera—Newton's optics, the emulsion film, the mini-computer. Truly remarkable. Yet some charcoal applied to paper by a single hand, nearly in the same manner as the cave artists of 40,000 years ago, commands a higher price than an entire roll of snapshots. Why?"

Mary flashes her usual lovely, crooked smile, considering for a moment as she collapses her tripod. Then she replies:

"But all the people who collaborated down the years on the camera aren't here in Jackson Square as Johnny snaps the shutter at Mom and Dad. Sure, mistakes and hesitations and choices went into the evolution of the camera, but all that creativity is hidden in history now."

She leans back, drifting further into the issue, giving her festoons a toss and placing one foot up against the iron fence that protects the great circle of petunias surrounding Jackson Square's inner park.

"On the other hand," she says, "my customers see choices, accidents, and corrections as I draw. The drawing is connected to fallibility and the moment. There are surprises waiting to happen with every drawing, and waiting to be discovered later by the viewer. So it's like life. It can always be changed in the process, and is never really finished . . . just sort of left off. Anyhow," she continues, coming back to the task of closing down shop, "I try to picture the customers in ways they'll like. I cook the books in their favor the way snapshots don't. Now tell me, Mr. Bijou, if you don't care for my drawings, why do you buy so many?"

"Oh I *do* like your work! That is not what I meant at all, not at all! And now I see why I love them. The sketch that I take home is the memory of a performance—of a graceful, magical performance."

"Well thank you! Listen, Mr. B, I gotta run. By the way, if

I don't see you again I want to thank you for buying all those drawings."

"What do you mean not see me again?"

"I'm getting married. We're moving to Boston. Dave is finishing a degree in archeology."

"But . . . what if there's a fire, or a car wreck?" Again he feels like a blundering actor inventing lines.

"What?"

"What I mean is, Mary, you were *born* in New Orleans."

"Things change, Mr. B. Life goes on."

"But are you sure it's the right decision, Mary? How will you know what to do there?"

"Well, we make it up as we go. You know what Roethke said: *I learn by going where I have to go*. I love that poem. Anyway, listen, thanks for your concern, but I gotta run. I've really enjoyed our talks."

Andre works his face into a goodbye smile, a smile that hardens for many moments, as though fixed with grade-school paste. He tries to find more to say but cannot. Mary fills the void by asking for his address, promising postcards and sketches from Boston.

On Sundays Andre usually buys a muffuletta at the Central Grocery to enjoy while watching *60 Minutes*. Today he forgets his muffuletta and walks, deep in thought, through the half-deserted streets of a late Sunday afternoon toward his apartment on Burgundy Street. In the distance he hears the clop of a donkey—no, a mule—perhaps Leon's trusty servant, pulling the day's last gaggle of tourists. From a doorway a dingy man, his face a filigree of broken veins, mutters and extends an unsteady hand. Andre pauses to fill it with coins.

Andre's morning rounds commenced beautifully with pastries and peaches, but then there was Mom's face invaded by noodles, her arm by an I.V. tube, and then the memory of Grandma drifting away in her plastic oxygen bubble. And now Mary singing the praises of change. Some things *do* change, Andre thinks. Interest rates fluctuate, microbes mutate. Station wagons disappeared and later there were SUVs. One day out of nowhere there was Velcro and missing kids on milk cartons. Spaghetti became pasta. Even in his own home, before her breast implants and the car wreck, Ruby had talked of marrying Sidney and moving to his house on Octavia Street, more than a mile away. But Andre has never known anyone who simply announced that she was moving to Boston. Hasn't she heard the song? Doesn't she know what it means to miss New Orleans?

Mary's decision to leave mingles in Andre's mind with what she said about drawing. What is so interesting about fallibility, about the possibility of choices and mistakes, about accidents and making it up as you go along? The good in life rests upon constancy—it is always finding the Croissant d'Or open in the morning, its full cast of pastries posed naughtily before you. It's seeing tourists emerge from the Café du Monde, each in a reverie of powdered sugar. It's always listening to Leon's patter behind the clip-clop of his trusty steed. It is finding one's bench on the levee, one's place in the scene. The art of living is nothing like Mary's precarious, slap-dash drawing, and if things change and mistakes are made, such smudges are certainly nothing to celebrate. The good life stays the same, like Coca-Cola. He is disappointed in Mary.

In the deep-sea light of early evening, Andre imagines that the Quarter is a sunken city and he is a diver searching for something lost and valuable, something that he can't name. By his doorstep, the wreckage of a Butterfinger protrudes from its wrapper. He enters the submerged chamber of his apartment, locking the doors behind him, the deadlock of the metal door snapping into its frame and the bolt of the wooden door sliding smoothly into its housing. He loves the Vieux Carre, but when it sinks into evening it's best to be safely inside and merely listen.

After hanging his red beret on the coat rack, Andre holds each of his three peaches to his nose, then arranges them in a row on top of the piano. He thinks of the three urns that will soon stand guard beneath Grandfather's portrait on Chestnut Street. Motionless in the middle of his living room, he is circled by pictures like the beads of a rosary. It is the gallery of his life, and the walls are crowded with Andre, each photo framed and blurred by dusty glass, blurred like Grandmother in her plastic bubble. Some are mere snapshots, others studio portraits. The exhibition has been arranged as a quasi-cinematic narrative, a montage timed to the pace of one's steps, which Andre has dubbed "Andre on the March" after the newsreel in *Citizen Kane*.

The wall to the right of the front door is a bustling nursery—a spanking new Andre seen through the glass of the hospital viewing room, baby Andre biding his time in his mother's arms, Andre with a pacifier plugged in his mouth. As today's Andre moves along the wall, the pictured Andre grows older—Andre under the live oak with his first red wagon, Andre and Ruby at the beach with buckets and shovels, Andre and a neighbor girl by the crepe myrtles wielding two of his father's golf clubs—"playing doctor," he used to say to tease his dad. And many more photos from the old days. Each picture is a shaving of time nicked off by the camera and preserved under glass.

Andre pauses by the stereo, lowering the needle to his recording of Moussourgsky's famous suite. Then he continues to the back wall, which offers scenes of Andre at Jesuit High School, where priests had encouraged him to imagine himself lifting a chalice before a throng of the faithful. And there are two blowups of Andre at Loyola University, one in which a grinning Andre holds his trophy for third in intramural golf, the other in which an Andre in green tights plays Puck in Marquette Theatre. Then, coming up the adjacent wall toward the front, the age of the pictured Andre approaches that of the viewing Andre. There are many scenes with elderly parents, two of him beside the coffin at Dad's funeral. Andre pauses to recall his father's dying words, his last performance, when life had struggled up from the clouded waters of his eyes. He had raised himself on one arm in the bedroom by the oak tree, had lifted the other into the air, and intoned in his deepest register:

"Marriage, my son! Marriage! You must look to the future. You must marry and play golf. Golf recapitulates our ancestral past, the wielding of weapons and the flight of projectiles. But the thrill of the sight of the flight of the ball also embodies our drive toward transcendence. The long ball hanging in the air is a figure of the future. Golf is the ultimate image of evolution, making copulation coherent."

Here Dad's speech had given way to a fit of coughing. Then he continued: "Like the next champion on the tee at Augusta, we must blast our genes through the winds of change and into the fresh and beckoning fairway of this new millennium. 'Tis generation only that dulls the Grim Guy's sickle and frosts the baleful balls of Death. So normal up, Andre! In the words of the immortal Dr. Freud, tee it up and get laid!"

Two days later Dad lay in a lacquered coffin, straight and proper as an Oscar—or a King Cobra driver.

After the funeral pictures, in a special place to the left of the front door, Mary's charcoal drawings converse among themselves. He is delighted by the fact that Mary has found various poses for him. In one his head is bare and he cradles his camera artistically, in another he wears his red beret at a jaunty angle, like Frank Sinatra, and in a third he carries his Sunday bag of fruit. In each drawing, Andre sits in a chair on the sidewalk by Jackson Square, the shops and restaurants receding into a background where people seem to hurry about their various lives. Some of these people are probably the accidents of art that Mary had spoken of—smudges disguised as intentions. And maybe, he thinks, people in the real world are only accidents in a larger composition. In any case, the people and the doorways in Mary's pictures trouble him now, as though the doorways are mysteries that others explore as he, quietly seated in the foreground, smiles blithely out into another world.

His thoughts of Mary mingle with a melody. Will he, too, be seeing her in all the old familiar places?

Stepping back to view the charcoals as a group, it occurs to him that the smudged background people are Andres he never became, parts that he turned down in life's drama. There, in one drawing, is Andre the businessman, scurrying along the street with a briefcase; there in another strolls Andre the lover, arm in arm with reproductive perfection. And perhaps the dark blur by the doorway in a third is Father Andre Bijou, S.J. In each drawing, lurking behind the central image of himself, he now sees a small gallery of once possible Andres.

As Moussorgsky ends, he realizes that his day and also his life have spiraled toward a still center like the grooves of a phonograph record. Would it have been worthwhile to have been more like the others, like those who colored inside the lines in school and who ran off to hide in grown-up jobs and families? If other lives change, why has he always just been Andre? Are these thoughts the surprises that Mary said were hidden in every drawing?

Sometimes Andre likes to reverse the gallery tour, running the film backwards to his birth. And often he thinks how sweet it would be to unlearn words and the world and to dwindle gently down and back into his young mother's arms, warm as morning pastry—and even more, to return to the dark and living warmth inside. But today there is no pleasure in this thought. Although *60 Minutes* has commenced, he merely stands for a long time, motionless in his living room, framed by the doorway and surrounded by his likenesses dozing in their frames. His film is over, and the moment flickers. The Vieux Carre is a lost city sinking deeper into the sea as the twilight air darkens and thickens around Andre and his other selves, newly discovered but already drowned. Then evening returns to the Vieux Carre like an old song.

Memories of
A Hypothetical Author

This is a memory of a memory. It concerns a drive that I took four years ago through Iowa, returning from Duluth and my new wife to New Orleans and the old job that I was about to quit—the reverse of the migration depicted in "Leaving Jenny." I 35 passes a few miles west of my home town in Minnesota. As the Civic glided by the old stomping grounds—we are all gliders, as Blake muses in his breakfast nook in Duluth—memories of earlier years meandered on stage, only to give way to ruminations on the then recent recovered-memory vs. false-memory imbroglio. I had just finished writing "The Night, the Stars," where I had given these same thoughts about memory to my disreputable protagonist. I had also given him some choice slices of my own life.

Freud feared that his patients' most traumatic memories were explanatory fictions, or myths of origin, fabricated by some inner gremlin hidden, like the Wizard of Oz, behind psychic curtains. Freud guardedly concluded that, for the purposes of therapy, the truth of these memories didn't matter. But for most purposes, truth does matter. We confer humanity upon one another because we know ourselves as repositories of storied experience, and the diseases and injuries that erase or revise memory are uniquely tragic. Each fissure in memory is a wound to the self.

Although we often seem oblivious to the past, repeating on Thursday the mistakes of Tuesday, culture and society are woven from memory. That courts have imprisoned people on the testimony of false memories is one instance of the importance of the memory problem. On a broader level, the ongoing conflict between official and alternative histories is another.

Setting the big issues aside, I'm glad to know that at least a few of my remembered idiocies and vulgarities, straggling back through the decades like Gretel's crumbs, may be only computer viruses of the mind. There's something oddly comforting in the notion of false memories, but it's a small comfort that drowns in the larger confusion. How do I know which of my crumbs of memory are real and which are apparitions? The false-memory thing resurrects Cartesian doubt from its academic graveyard. If my memories are suspect, who or what am "I"? How do I find my way home?

I like to write short stories because it eases the anxiety attending that "I" question. In fiction, fact and make-believe are allowed to share a bed, somewhat the way Pablo Neruda is allowed to walk around in a skirt in "Pablo and I." In fiction, the normal rules of propriety take a hike. It's great that Charlotte Bronte winnowed and ground and baked her memories into a novel, and no one demands autobiographical accuracy. We accept the fact that Hemingway, whose mother dressed him as a girl, re-accessorized himself on the page with guns and battle scars. Writers of fiction get to make things up and to stretch the rest, just as two of my characters (their imaginings are cribbed from a story by my old colleague, John Biguenet) dream of stretching their bodies into heroic shapes.

There is truth in lies, as Aristotle taught us in *Poetics*. We suppose that the personal essay embraces autobiography, but even here, where the intent is both representational and expressive, memories are auditioned, scrubbed, and costumed for the show. The most intricate documentation cannot ensure authenticity, and the inability of writing to authenticate itself is at once writing's scandal and its fascination. Personal writing may well be the outted secret of the illusionary Self.

As I neared Des Moines in my Civic, these thoughts ducked in and out of the scenery, along with some low-level brooding over old blunders and my currently divided life. The distance from Duluth to New Orleans, a sporadic motif in the stories in this collection, is not merely geographic, and our minds don't change addresses as easily as our tables and chairs. It would be hot in New Orleans, with half of the Gulf of Mexico sloshing around in the air, as Hugh says in his story. Before plunging back into that overly-hydrated world, I needed a therapeutic walk in the country, and a Motel 6 obligingly appeared around a bend.

The office was personed by a well-ornamented young woman with fingernails as long as lobster tails and a nose that attempted a risky, but more or less successful, imitation of a buzzard's beak. Her blouse had a metallic shine that might reflect death rays. In truth, she seemed to be a well-sampled lollipop. I conducted my business, then headed down the sidewalk toward the stairs. I'm skinny—with a touch of my own buzzardliness—and bent with the weight of my duffel bag I must have looked like a fishing pole that has snagged a boot.

The stairs began at the far side of the swimming pool, a small, blighted concavity of green cement in whose chlorinated and fishless water three or four kids splashed about under the sporadic glances of parents camped in deck chairs. I paused at the pool entrance, setting down my bag in preparation for the climb. A strategically placed sign displayed the rules and regulations governing one's chlorine dip. Following a number of specific offenses—running, pushing, swearing, and boozing—came the horseplay prohibition, a prohibition that has always worked about as well with children as the capitalized Prohibition worked with adults.

The horseplay injunction began its chemistry in the memory vat. Decades ago, I chased and tumbled my way through childhood in the Minnesota farm town called Wanamingo. When I was inventing a childhood for Blake, the guy who is haunted in the corners of his eyes, I took Wanamingo and moved it to Iowa, changing its name on the way—a bit of redistricting to outdo even the Texas Republicans.

In any case, when I was a child there in the Forties, sixty miles from the fabled sophistication of the Twin Cities, *horseplay* was a hopelessly old-fashioned word, a word in dark flannel trousers that was uttered by nagging grandparents (I lived with my grandparents then) who were made uneasy by at least half of what it was fun for kids to do in those days before Velcro and video cams. No matter what my scheme—my projected gopher-breeding business, the hole in the roof that I planned for a telescope—my grandparents said *no*. They had *no* down pat. *No, Bruce, I don't think so. No, dear, it just isn't practical. Not today. No. No.* If kids were accused of horseplay, the grownups lived lives of interminable neigh-saying.

In the 1930s, Wilder Penfield used electrical stimuli to elicit apparent memories in his patients, but these memories turned out to be constructs cobbled together from random fragments of the previous day's experiences—electrically induced short stories. Similarly, the horseplay sign might have elicited the memory that I've just reported, which may have been reshaped by the writing process and its thirst for effect, writing having roughly the same relation to experience as bodybuilding has to real work. Although false memories in prose can add up to Aristotle's crooked truth, I should clarify that my grandparents, the Olsons, were good to me in difficult times.

My grandmother—her name was Lillian but we called her Nana—is always old in my recollection, battling weeds on her knees in the garden, marching me to church on Sundays, or coming with cookies in the evening in clothes that rustle like autumn leaves. We'd sit on lawn chairs in the early evening, listening to the German shepherd down the block, tethered to a post and eager for a meal and a few pats, invoke the failing light with his repertoire of yips, howls, and whines. Then, as a breeze sighed contentedly, Nana would tell family stories, pausing to return the waves of people crunching by in their cars on the gravel road. A drive-by was a friendly thing then.

And that faint vibrato in the air as darkness came—was it the stars?

Nana was in charge of the family's official memory. There are two kinds of memory—the official kind enshrined in photo albums, newspaper clippings, and in the stories that Nana told on summer evenings or at holiday dinners. Then there is the private stuff, the individual memories that each of us keeps tucked away in a different room. We're all equipped with varying proportions of these two kinds of mismatched furniture.

My grandmother's memory was so powerful that she could recall things whether they had happened or not. An example of an official memory was Nana's version of the morning that we all rose before the sun to drive to Zumbrota to meet Uncle Conley, who was returning from WWII by bus. Authority has it that I rubbed sleep from my eyes—I would have been four years old then—and inquired, in reference to a sartorial gift from a rich aunt, "Mrs. Eitel's suit, I presume?" To make matters worse, when Grandpa's Ford crested a hill just as the sun bubbled up over the horizon, Nana insists that my oozing rapture included, "What is this prettiness that I see all around me?"

I don't remember committing either of these betrayals of boyhood, and if I had heard such stuff from a friend I would have jammed frogs down his shirt. But submitting to these stories at Thanksgiving or Christmas was the price that I paid for my pumpkin pie or my stocking stuffed with Milky Ways. Like those hapless prisoners of later years, I was branded by a memory that just *had* to be wrong. But on some small, involuntary level, I presume, I still wear the suit woven from the pretty threads of official history that I heard all around me at Nana's house.

Uncle Conley, by the way, had been a pacifist during his school days at Carlton College in Northfield, MN, but he was converted to the war effort, perhaps by Pearl Harbor. I'm traveling a similar road. For most of my life I have not wished to kill anyone with whom I have not had personal dealings, and I was a peacenik during the Vietnam years. I'm mindful of the danger of letting terrorists corrupt our values, but recent events have caused me to become more generous with my murderous inclinations.

Conley's father and my grandfather, Frederick Olson, was the town doctor. In the early days he made calls to farms across the snow-bandaged roads and fields in a sleigh pulled by a horse, and later, during the Depression, he accepted payment in eggs or handshakes. He spent his final years institutionalized with dementia.

About a decade ago, my mother gave me a crumpled letter from his final years, dictated to a nurse, in which he pleads with Nana to take him home. It is the saddest thing that I've ever read. I know nothing of Nana's response, which has escaped official memory—another of those gliders that slip around in the wings. Grandpa stayed in the hospital in St. Cloud. I did not observe his slide from kindness to senility, although I must certainly have been obliviously present. I've been told, and I believe, that in his entire career he never sent a bill. That is how the town remembers him—or did, since much time has passed—and how I choose to as well.

Once, on the front porch, I struck Grandpa in the stomach with my kid-sized baseball bat, the only tantrum of that sort that I remember throwing. I don't know what led up to it—maybe the denied telescope, but it may have happened in another summer altogether. In any case, Nana assured me that my tantrum would bring me a comeuppance, and I believed her.

Nana was an authority on comeuppance—the Queen of Comeuppance. Comeuppance was her study and her passion. She could name all those in town who had one coming, and she watched vigilantly for its approach to their doorsteps. The other morning I woke up with the notion that *The Wanamingo Progress* had run a comeuppance column somewhere between the weddings and obituaries, and that Nana had authored it. But that was just memory goofing around again.

I don't know what followed my swing at Grandpa. Memories blur on either side. But the isolated event, surgically removed from time, stays with me as a reminder of my potential to do harm. In any case, Grandfather and Nana were good people in a way of life that is gone now.

My mother was a single mom, which was no walk in the park in those days. A hospital nurse in Austin (I passed by Austin on my way down I 35), where she rented a room, she would come home when she could to her parents' Dutch colonial house on the edge of Wanamingo (a town of 450 is mostly edges), and our sessions with the Oz books were my introduction to joy and wonder. We'd sit on the bed or by the fireplace in the living room, scrunched together to admire the illustrations—I remember Rinkatink best, plump and jolly on the cover of his volume. An officious grandfather clock stood at attention in the living room, and it was strange to be summoned back from Oz by the sound of time passing in Wanamingo.

We read the entire, dusty collection of first editions, or at least, when we visited in later years, we told one another that we read them all. That was our story, and I'm sticking to it. My mother has become demented, and it's impossible to share these memories with her now. The Oz books were stored unceremoniously in a battered trunk in the attic next to an old rifle with a bayonet—Grandpa had served in WWI. Years later, Mom told me that the books were eventually donated to a library in the nearby town of Canon Falls, where Aunt (pronounced Ant) Millie was the librarian. I dimly recall a waggish relative at family reunions calling her Shush.

Besides Aunt Mill, I remember a few relatives of grandpa's generation, especially his brothers Glen and Lorie, but, to tell the truth, I've never had much interest in the ancestors and would make a damn poor Native American. The family photo albums have gone to my cousins, who remain in touch with the shadowy celebrities of the past. I've never had a desire to look at old pictures that couldn't be overcome by the prospect of a long walk or a game of eight ball.

Compared to my mom, my father was a thoroughly different story, or more accurately a scattering of stories torn from the pages of pulp fiction. By the start of my remembered life (I was born in '41, a few months before we joined the war), he had already drunk and caroused himself out of our lives and into others, returning from time to time like the repressed memories that Freud spoke of, troubling the ponds and coves of my childhood. I've often wondered, when nights grow late enough, what became of him, but his journey, devoted to the steamier regions of what we euphemistically call the private life, was too disreputable for official memory. He's the father that Hugh recalls in "The Night, the Stars" and that Blake recalls in "Gliders."

He sidestepped the fatherhood blitz, and Nana's diplomacy limped off the field. Hearing her speak of him made me think of something falling into an abandoned well, splashing in dark, obscene waters. It is hard to remember him without suspecting that I'm inventing. He's mostly just a vapor trail—one of those gliders who float in and out of the lives of more solid people. He was a liar and a thief, and the father, no doubt, of many of my insecurities.

Anyway, in those warm Wanamingo days, when the Oz books dozed in their box and Mrs. Eitel's suit sulked in the closet, my pals and I leapt hedges, kicked through Olaf Johnson's freshly raked leaves, and stole raspberries and rhubarb from Mrs. Haugan's—Gwen Haugan's—garden. Sometimes a screen door would slam. We'd lift our heads like wary deer, then return to our grazing. You crushed raspberries against the ceiling of your mouth with your tongue, feeling the purple drupelets separate and slide into a sweet nectar. But rhubarb was tough. You bit into it and pulled, face scrunched and eyes squeezed shut, leaving vanquished fibers dangling from the stalk in your hand. Rhubarb pie was one of my grandmother's specialties, but I didn't take to it. What was good about rhubarb was stealing it.

With some memories you're a detached audience, gathering wool in the cheap seats—the self keeping a sanitary distance from its remembered object. With other memories you seem once again to join yesterday's fray. The old feelings blow through you like wind in a tree, and you're physically transported. Again you taste rhubarb from childhood's garden or watch the sun settle on gaudy wings behind the West Woods over a half a century ago. Again the thrill flashes along your spine as you look into the night sky circa 1949, and the twinkle of the stars mingles with the chirrup of the crickets until it is the stars that chirrup and the crickets are little worlds just there in the lilacs and the elms. And you hear the plangent call of the train whistle far away. Maybe this physical participation argues for the authenticity of the memory, although the visceral sensations might be so many special effects that the false-memory gremlin produces to enhance its fictions.

But I swear that we chewed rhubarb like pitchers chew tobacco or bubble gum, and more than one garage window around town shattered even before the finish of a big-league follow through. We'd light out, shrieking like the noon whistle, off to practice other skills of boyhood—maybe the armpit fart (a cinch), the ear wiggle (a tough one), the fingers-in-the-mouth whistle *(please,* dear God, show me the way). Or we'd practice cursing under the expert guidance of Davy Weaver, who claimed that his great-grandfather had been the first person to move to Wanamingo. Davy could stuff the joints of the smallest sentence with so much profanity that it exploded into a field of rubble, and he was adept at modulating the volume and intonation of his expletives to match all emergencies. He provided me with an auxiliary vocabulary, replete with performance pointers, that has severed well to this day.

We were an unphilosophical bunch, unable to focus on the problem of a town pre-existing its first inhabitant, so Davy's ancestral claim stood. He was democratically minded, though, and accepted the rest of us as only slightly inferior beings. I have met many similar people since, descendants of fat insurance policies and agile businesses, and none were more likeable than Davy.

Nana always wondered how Davy turned out so ratty, since his parents were so proper. My guess is that some folks are nurtured into arrogance along the way, but others hit the planet arrogant from the git-go, no assembly needed. That was Davy. Evolution may have taught us that friendliness has survival value, but it's also taught that arrogance and nastiness pay off too, at least sometimes. So I think Davy's qualities were selected by the species in the old Darwinian yard sale and can't be blamed on his timid, churchy parents.

But he was a good instructor, and we practiced the arts of cursing and ear-wiggling with wary eyes, since around every corner lurked an adult, perhaps made stern by the war, packing a horseplay lecture under his feed cap. As a more pointed antidote to Davy's vocabulary lessons, there was one old codger whose discourse was an endless parade of words like whosoever and thee, words like streetlights on the road to salvation. Once, after a particularly long sermon from this personage, Davy had the temerity to scoff, using his most pyrotechnic language, at the very idea of religion itself. The following winter he broke his toe sledding on Bakko's hill, sending at least one of his followers back into the waiting arms of the Trinity Lutheran Church, where legendary characters in leaded glass inspected him with jaundiced eyes.

Nonetheless, horseplay remained something we kids knew nothing about. We bridled at the word. Once, after an especially dynamic dressing down, Marvin Carlson, who was simple and wore a permanent grin like a Jack-o'-lantern, muttered: *cripes, horses were here first*. This bit of obscure wisdom became our mantra. Now, at an Iowa Motel 6, decades down time's interstate, I imagined that the sign by the pool had been planted especially for me by some latter-day Mnemosyne, now a moronic motel deity fumbling for ways to make a stack of bedrooms seem like home. If Proust had shown up in a Peugot, there would have been madeleines in his room.

Of course memory is an idiot, tossing aside much that might have been useful and enriching—like the difference between volts and amps, or Holsteins and Guernseys—while embalming for the remainder of one's life the smell of a cookie, Davy's broken toe, or the words of Marvin Carlson. Go figure.

After plopping my bag down on the bureau before a cracked mirror, I went for my walk, passing a small band of teenaged boys coming and going on the balcony with mandatory Buds in hand (perhaps the madeleines of *their* futures), on the road in fine Kerouac tradition and high-fiving like there was no tomorrow. I found my own road, one that extended out behind the motel, first past a row of houses, then a nursery, and then a sod farm. It was a lovely summer afternoon; the air was garrulous with insects and the sinking sun had a nostalgic look in its eye.

There is a poem by James Wright called "A Blessing" in which he stops by a roadside near Pine Island, which is about fifteen miles from Wanamingo. In Wright's poem two horses come to the fence, and as he strokes them "they bow shyly as wet swans." Then, in the twilight breeze, he realizes that "if I stepped out of my body I would break into blossom." As I walked by the sod farm in Iowa, I wanted to see horses. I also wished that James Wright were still with us. I took a Shakespeare class from him at the University of Minnesota, and his occasional intimations of a deep, personal sadness moved me.

Years later, through a happy chance, I enjoyed oysters and trout with James and his wife, Anne, in New Orleans. He died in the Eighties of the same kind of throat cancer that I had resected a few months before my drive back to Minnesota. I suppose the Powers That Be decided that they needed another poet in the Afterworld, but I wish that they had found a gentler form of conveyance for such a gentle man. And I hope the Powers appreciate his society, since his original, earthly readers are mostly out to pasture now.

At the far end of the field, as the hum and clatter of the freeway faded away, the road turned west into a country lane with lovely old houses on either side, houses with sprawling lawns populated with willows and cedars and flower gardens. Children in the yards said hello and I returned the greeting with waves, careful not to take too great an interest. A stranger around kids should keep walking, and as I walked Susan Lagerstrom skipped onto memory's playground.

She was my girlfriend in the sixth grade. Mom and I had left Wanamingo to see the world, the world being the Twin Cities of Minneapolis and St. Paul. By the sixth grade, I had wandered from the rhubarb and lilacs of Wanamingo to St. Paul, to Minneapolis, to what is now one of its suburbs, Eden Prairie, then across the country to Utah, and then again out to Long Beach, California, where my father appeared as if by black magic. With only the ocean to the west, Mom and I hung a new water bag from the radiator and pointed the blue Kaiser at Minneapolis. Perhaps, when one can no longer outrun the past, one goes home. It was good to be back in Minneapolis, where Susan's curls bounced about her face like the paper festoons that you'd break off and throw at birthday parties.

She was an artist and into horses big time. Gallant steeds with wind-blown manes reared and plunged across the pages of her Big Chief tablet and her school notebooks, stampeding through diagrammed sentences, rearing at the sight of a denominator, and grazing among decision trees and pie charts. She could talk roans and bays, stallions and mares, quarter horses and Clydesdales. She once confided to me, as we peeled our Popsicles one bright summer day in the doorway of Mr. Elvy's Dairy Store at 54th and Penn, that her bedroom, a palace of galloping dreams, was papered by her own hand into a single, whinnying collage.

We kissed once in her backyard, the old lady next door gawking as if we were theater in the park. I tried to regret our rash deed for a few days, but fortunately I was unsuccessful. A few years down the trail I became an aficionado of the dalliance alfresco, but most of all, memory's eye still sees Susan's little lips puckered into a happy starburst under the maple tree.

And further on that trail, at the U of M, I spent evenings with another Sue discussing the newest authors—writers such as William Styron and John Updike—over contraband beers. *Lie Down in Darkness* and *Rabbit, Run* were my introduction to the fiction of my own time in those salad days, when Proust rhymed with Faust and one pronounced the ess in Camus. Before long I found myself following the glimmer of the lit. bug. Physics, where I had started at the university, seemed to be all weapons and missiles back then. Those were good days, but as someone said, folks long to go on pilgrimages. What he didn't say is that folks often don't return anytime soon. Time, though, can spread all the deep water it wants, I can still see Sue—both of my lovely Sues—smiling on the far shore.

I had been recently remarried at the time of my drive back to New Orleans. My spouse *du jour*, as an old friend insisted on calling her, lives on a hillside in Duluth. In the morning, from her breakfast nook, you can watch the sun rise over Lake Superior and, in the winter, the branches of the pines all down the hill fill with pillows of snow. It's the scene that Blake broods over in "Gliders."

Snow falling from an upper branch, gently colliding with lower branches and sifting finally to the ground, images the mind falling back through time, as it is likely to do from the height of a certain age. But my memories of Minnesota, its gravitational pull, had a more immediate purpose that day in Iowa. They lent me an identity and a future as I drove back to the sodden streets of New Orleans to quit a job and put some things in order.

My wife's name is Viki. We married a month before my surgery, and in spite of her parenting duties she came to New Orleans to spend six surreal weeks with me in Lakeside Regional Medical Center on the north side of Lake Pontchartrain. Viki slept wedged in a flop-out chair by my bed. She noticed the dehiscence of my surgical wound during the third week. The nurse on duty didn't think it was an issue, but Viki insisted on calling the doctor. Within the hour I had the privilege of lying beneath the floodlights again. Later the surgeon told me that Viki had saved my life, and I love her more than stolen berries.

But it was Dr. Sabatier, Richard, who did the work under the lights and by his great skill, and character too, reinserted life to whatever room it rents in my hotel of bone, flesh, and blood. Richard's visits to my hospital room ran to an hour or more as he delivered himself of medical anecdotes and political opinions. Whatever the value of the latter, his attention lent my wife and me the feeling of actually being important to him, a crucial aspect of his art. Because of Richard's success, my expertise concerning the hereafter is diminished, but I think that dying is a mundane thing and not nearly the spooky event that folks make it out to be.

Viki and I had known each other as children in Minneapolis, although her version of those days differs from mine. Our conspiring mothers, still friends, arranged a surprise reunion after our respective marriages went belly-up. Viki and I were in our forties then, finding ourselves once again in debt to parental wisdom and trickery.

Viki has a way with food, and although I have always steered clear of kitchens, she swears that she was making progress with me for a time. The woman's job, she says, is to civilize the male. But I don't even eat Popsicles now, having lost my epiglottis during my vacation in Lakeside Regional. Once the rhubarb years of

Wanamingo were completely behind me, I came to like my Luckies and my Coors, and the body is a strict accountant—another kind of memory.

I have a small barrel implanted in my abdomen, and at the promptings of hunger or thirst I simply lift my shirt, attach a funnel to the barrel, and pour in whatever's at hand. The whole arrangement, which I recommend to the world at large, saves many tedious hours of trudging the aisles of supermarkets, waiting over oven timers, and dawdling over salads, pastas, and cakes and pies. But I'd still eat Popsicles if I could, along with Dreamsicles, Pushups, and Drumsticks (later called Nutty-Buddies), and I'd never trust a person who has willingly abandoned these icy, summertime delights. How could there be a soul in such a one?

I'm sure that my recent gastronomical arrangements, like El Nino, have worked changes in my psychic weather. Food, in memory and in fantasy, is an ingredient of one's self concept. Fantasies of financial windfalls include ordering Oysters Rockefeller at Commander's Palace, while romantic imaginings require candlelight, a split of chilled champagne and Beluga caviar (it's as hard to be a good environmentalist in one's fantasy life as in one's real life). Besides the rhubarb and berries, Wanamingo memories are dabbed with mustard and ketchup and rest on a firm foundation of "hot dish," a low-rent, Minnesota casserole made of canned peas and mushroom soup and whatever else yesterday graciously left behind.

During the early days in Minneapolis, before the move to Utah, my mother and I lived in a snailback trailer parked in an alley near Minnehaha Park. These days were a recurring banquet of Spam sandwiches and Hormel chili, all you could eat. Later, when we had our little house on Upton Avenue, the hormonal stirrings that soon blundered me into the life of the second Sue were caused, I'm positive, by Beek's combination pizza. And further down life's culinary highway, my grad school days in Los Angeles were sustained by tuna and bean sprouts. Each pit stop has its menu, and now, while Viki looks helplessly on, I pour into my tube a manufactured concoction called Jevity. Clearly, I shouldn't be held responsible for recent behavioral changes.

And it must be Jevity's fault that as soon as I try to represent myself, or my selves, whether on paper or in conversation, they seem not to coincide with the real me, as though consciousness and identity aren't even batting in the same ballpark. I'm uneasy when I hear that someone's personal writings are being used against him in court, as in the Ted Kaczynski case a few years ago. The relationship between the composed self that appears on paper and the self that walks the streets is too problematic. This fissure may be, as Marxists would say, symptoms of social contradictions. Thomas Jefferson owned slaves and wrote the Declaration of Independence; Charles Dickens sentimentalized the family in print but was a scalawag in London.

Today desire explodes in all directions, looking for the action. It's pasties and G-strings, a vast striptease, and one life just isn't enough. As Pablo's new friend says, the "I" that seems so singular and erect on the page often feels more like an urban site of perpetual demolition and reconstruction. The "self," I think, is always hypothetical. I smile when oldsters ask children what they want to be when they grow up—the answers will certainly be as off the mark as old science fiction. We don't live intended lives.

As a young man I struck a lot of poses trying to outlive my small-town origins. Like many guys under thirty, the computer in my skull was equipped with a powerful firewall that repelled most of the reason and wisdom with which my elders besieged it. Any that got through was deleted like spam. Maybe even on that day in Iowa, thinking about my home town while the jazz clubs of New Orleans beckoned, I was having it both ways. I strike deals with reality, and the emergence of a coherent, finished person doesn't seem to be in the cards. Maybe we spend so much time becoming that we forget to be.

But writing fiction is a way to orchestrate and even enjoy the confusion by venturing out of the one life that you're stuck with. At the very least, fictionalizing is good therapy for a recovering academic, although I sometimes wonder if my ilk should not also have its own AA. To become an academic, I earned a degree called a Ph.D. I understand this to mean that I am a Doctor of Philosophy, although I've never prescribed cures to anyone else's philosophy, having maimed my own with too much cosmetic surgery.

These days, neurologists report that the brain is always reorganizing itself, as perhaps it did for Blake in "Gliders." I imagine sparks bursting in the dark recesses of cells and jetting along in ever-shifting patterns of nerves like a constantly changing fireworks display. Probably I've got the imagery all wrong, but the idea is that there is a physiological basis for the morphing of memories and of personality.

Be that as it may, Wanamingo is really there, dreaming itself into existence off the road to Rochester, spreading a bit with passing time, and carrying its own backpack of human history, not unlike its individual inhabitants. I've driven through it a few times in recent years, stopping at the cemetery that presides from a hill to the north, remembering my grandparents and trying to imagine their parents, who came from Norway and Sweden to farm this land. Or trying to imagine my mother's youth, on its way to a bad marriage and to motherhood in that small town while the world wobbled between wars. And there are Indian mounds not far from the cemetery, evoking another history, other joy and sadness.

Then I point the car down the hill straight at the water tower, put it in neutral, and coast past the creamery and the grain elevator and into town as Mom and I did when visiting from Minneapolis in my grade-school days. If you carried some speed over the hill and the wind was right, you could almost creep to Romness's Restaurant, which held down the north end of Main Street. We'd go to Romness's one night a week when I lived with my grandparents, not on Saturdays out of consideration for the farmers who would come to town. Space was limited. During the summer, town kids didn't go for a haircut on Saturday either.

We would sit in a booth at Romness's and I'd order "two hamburgers with onions, mustard, and ketchup and milk to drink," my unvarying words that soon became part of the fabric of Nana's official memory. If you didn't specify the fixings, you'd just get the disk of meat on a bun, maybe a pickle chip. You'd wander past Romness's with a chum on a summer afternoon and fish in your pocket for a nickel for a Dreamsicle, finding perhaps a fugitive Milk Dud gathering lint. And a few doors down, in front of Bill's Saloon, the town drunk would be searching his own pockets, spittle dribbling into a beard as large as a rain forest. You'd steal a look at his ravaged eyes and hurry on.

There is still a restaurant at the edge of town, but it sports a different name now—something cute no doubt, as it's just down the block from a new "solon" called Hair Port. In my drinking days in New Orleans I knew a guy who tried to put together investors for a brothel to be called Come As You Are. But I digress.

I'd put the car in gear and drift by the restaurant again, an old guy with out-of-state plates, heading for the street I had lived on. A few years ago I stopped to chat with Gwen, who edited the weekly newspaper, *The Wanamingo Progress*, for what seemed like decades. Gwen had been our next-door neighbor, and she was a repository of town history.

Her father had been a journalist in the oral tradition, one who would gladly tell you all he knew and even more. It was years later that I realized how much he resembled Mark Twain, with a huge moustache holding down his upper lip like a paper weight, concealing smiles and lending a gruff appearance that was the perfect foil for his drollery. He'd hunker down on the front step, old as Norway, shift his eyes into a five-mile gaze, and tell you about times such as the winter of '41, my birth year: *Yeah, that was a cold one. Why, you'd go to milk the cow and it'd come slipping out froze solid like the Pushups you kids buy at Romness.*

Only these were Pushdowns, if you see what I mean.

He's been gone a long time now, taking his own place among fabled snows. As Gwen and I talked that day a few years back, her voice crackling softly now like newspaper gone brittle in the bottom of a trunk, I wondered what tales have been told to subsequent generations of credulous kids, and if other sneakered soldiers (Reeboks or Nikis now, not Keds) have been forced by the cruelties of imagined wars to plunder her compound for rhubarb, gooseberries, and raspberries. And I wonder what they will remember, each with his own Wanamingo.

For my part, I don't know if, on my walk in Iowa, I remembered these things exactly as I write them now. This writing is a memory of memories, and would be doubly suspect were writing not a place where all is allowed. James Wright has a poem called "Milkweed" in which he remembers a moment from the past when a memory moved him deeply, but he cannot say what it was. The poem creates a memory of a forgetting: *Whatever it was I lost, whatever I wept for / Was a wild, gentle thing.* I think that much writing is like that—however it was, this is how it seems to me now. The postmodernists talked (they, to, recede into the past) about grand narratives and little histories, suggesting that the tireless spinning of narratives is the essential human and cultural activity.

As I walked along in Iowa, my momentary half-way house between Duluth and New Orleans, a power mower buzzed in the early evening, accompanying the occasional troupes of gnats that accosted me on the country road. Butterflies flickered over hedges like shavings of polished agate. Above the gardens and yards, swallows darted for insects, catching fast food on the wing, and occasionally a dog ambled around the side of a house for a look-see. There was one whose society I enjoyed for a couple of minutes, a chocolate lab who was all lovely eyes, wiggles, and warm suede. And further off, behind the houses, friendly old hills leaned together like cattle, just as other hills had as you looked out to the countryside from Bakko's Hill in Wanamingo's cerulean summers.

The Midwestern sunset was lovely that day in Iowa, spread across the horizon like crushed berries. Wandering back toward the motel and minding my middle-aged business, I remembered again the steeplechases over the neighbors' hedges and the scrambling, sliding races down Bakko's Hill to the swimming hole in the creek, sans chlorine and deck chairs and posted rules, but dashed with shiners and the occasional frog. After a swim, you'd sit on the bank with your skin turned to Braille by the icy water, and you'd slowly warm as the afternoon sun flung gold coins across the creek. Perhaps you'd see a green snake vanish through the grass by your feet like a thread pulled from a tapestry.

At the motel pool, a solitary man sporting a shaggy beard, thoroughly broiled and plump with success or bad food, gathered together his radio, towel and lotions. Then, for an instant, the stairway by the pool in Iowa almost became the turning staircase in my grandparents' home, with the step that creaked and the smooth banister under my hand. My room waited at the far end of the hall, under the attic with its box of dreams. When the wind blew, a gnarled old elm rapped his knuckles on my bedroom wall like some traveler returned from The Gnome Kingdom of Oz. In the patient mornings, I'd awaken from time to time like a fish breaking water, only to swim back into the caves and grottos of dreamspace.

The next morning in Iowa, I cleared the bureau and stuffed a few things back into my duffel bag, my image sloshing about in the mirror, back and forth across the crack that slanted diagonally like a jagged line on a graph. The high-fivers on the balcony had vamoosed, and the kids with their semi-watchful parents at the pool were gone, tugged by private forces out there in America—family, jobs, maybe dreams of adventure and glory. The green cavity yawned vacantly, and the horseplay interdiction loomed in wait of the next intrusion of wayfaring malefactors.

Following the instructions posted by my door, I dropped the key at the office, where the person with the belobstered hands had been replaced by a matronly woman rich in powder and poundage. A necklace of small, amber stones was like a row of ants exploring the folds of flesh that drooped to her shoulders. Above her smeared lipstick and huge, clip-on earrings, her gray hair fell about her head like a well-used dish towel. All of it testifying to the futility, after a certain age, of adornment.

I hoisted my bag into the Civic, swung onto the entrance ramp, and continued the long drive to New Orleans, feeling profoundly less free on the freeway than I had on the country road. Settled behind the wheel, I wondered if the days of the real walking tour were over, the kind that people like Angel Clare took in Victorian novels, and if walking itself has become an art practiced by a dwindling few. Perhaps in the future even our parks will have moving sidewalks.

Not that I've ever had, in Thoreau's phrase, a genius for sauntering—he speculates that the word might be related to *sans terre*, without a fixed place. My strolls are occasional, sporadic events, and I've been too much *sans terre*—gliding away in autos and airplanes—to find the concept romantic. Watching the fall migration of hawks from Hawk Ridge in Duluth fills me with loneliness. I'm not a wilderness man. Probably because of the dislocations of my childhood, I'm touched most deeply by habitable places—places where gliders can rest.

Whatever it was I lost, whatever I wept for
Was a wild, gentle thing.

I'm not a wilderness man, but sometimes I'm a country-road man. A country road is a place between the city and the wilderness, the freeway and the deer path. It can offer prospects and perspectives upon the lives that we live together in relation to nature and across time. A country road offers fields beyond a nursery haunted by horses from a dead man's poem, and by pictures of horses drawn by a childhood friend. It can offer a model of lives together in the present, of peaceful homes with gardens of delphiniums and day lilies, impatiens and petunias, homes with kids in the yards who say hello to a stranger.

About The Author

Bruce Henricksen's short stories have appeared in numerous literary magazines, including *Arts & Letter, The Briar Cliff Review, Edge City Review, Folio, New Orleans Review, North Dakota Quarterly, Palo Alto Review,* and *Southern Humanities Review*. One of his stories is the lead piece in *French Quarter Fiction* (Light of New Orleans Publishing, 2003), an anthology that includes work by some of America's best known authors. This volume was named the Book of the Year in 2003 by the Gulf South Booksellers Association. His piece in the anthology *Mota 4: Integrity* (Triple Tree Publishing) was nominated for a Pushcart Prize, and his short story collection was a finalist for the St. Lawrence Book Award, the Serena McDonald Kennedy Award, and the Grace Paley Prize for Short Fiction.

Bruce taught writing and literature at Loyola University New Orleans, where he chaired the English Department and edited *New Orleans Review*. His academic writing includes a study of Joseph Conrad, *Nomadic Voices: Conrad and the Subject of Narrative* (University of Illinois Press, 1992), and *Murray Krieger and Contemporary Critical Theory* (Columbia University Press, 1986). He lives in Duluth MN with his wonderful wife, Viki.

A reader's guide for this book is available at:
www.brucehenricksen.com